The Madness

JARALE PHILLIPS

This book has no editor.

It is better to remain silent, and be thought insane, than to write a book and remove all doubt.

"But when we came into this strange land, pure praise was no longer ours, nor righteous prayer, nor understanding hearts, nor sweet thoughts... neither is our bright nature left us. But our body is changed from the similitude in which it was at first, when we were created."

-The first book of Adam and Eve

Your Narrator, An Introduction

GOOD AFTERNOON to you my most trusted reader, and my sincerest apology if you've made the decision to begin this journey in the wake of an early morning, or slip of night. You must know that I myself have consumed the inner cover of many a work at all conceivable hours, and hold no grudge toward anyone starting this particular offering at the time that best suits them. In fact, I first embarked on Gil Scot-Heron's *The Vulture* while alone in my apartment at 2:43am.

I'd been up all night trying to come down from a PCP-laced joint gifted to me by a former associate, and the silky smooth literary style of Mr. Scott-Heron was able to guide my frazzled mind into some semblance of working order.

It is with sadness that I must admit to you, trusted reader, that in spite of my best efforts I will in all likelihood be incapable of doing for you what our friend Gil did for me that troublesome morning. The reasons for this are several, and I do hope to gain your understanding in my explanation.

Firstly you must be made aware that I, your narrator, am quite mad. So much so that I am crafting the very words you read from the confines of a madhouse. It is of course my moral, and, as I've been told, legal obligation to inform you of my current condition, so there you have it.

As a result, the subsequent stories upon which your eyes

shall soon feast will undoubtedly be a bit frayed, scattered, and, one might even say, twisted.

It is my personal advisement that if you find yourself to be heavily impressionable, sensitive, or squeamish in nature, that you close this book at once and do your best to forget of its existence. You might find it useful to dig a proper hole so that you may bury your physical copy, or perhaps gift it to a person for whom you do not have particularly fond feelings.

At any rate, be warned that what you are presently in possession of are the thoughts of a madman, and one thing I can tell you from experience is that madness is highly contagious.

The second confession I must burden you with, trusted reader, is that while I do consider myself a writer, I am technically, or rather literally incapable of performing the physical act. A few years ago I achieved the rare feat of severing both hands from my body without the aid of any outside assistance. It was a daunting task which, while having earned the great esteem of my housemates, has managed to handicap quite a few of my most joyous pastimes.

The words you read now are being dictated by me to my two-handed bunkmate, who is choosing to remain nameless throughout this process. What I can tell you, however, is that he's quite famous for murdering a large number of people, and, if you are anything like me, you will find it admirable that throughout the course of his career he never made his way to a single child, or person above the age of seventy-one.

A bit less impressive is his unwillingness to edit, or rewrite my savory tales, hence the faux pas regarding time of day just a moment ago.

Still, you may rest assured that you are in the very capable would-be hands of a master in the art of story. We won't let a little thing like editing get in our way, now will we?

In fact, if you've made it this far without turning away, my guess is that you aren't much of a stickler at all when it comes to following rules. Am I right? Of course I am. And since you and I are of the same sadistic mindset, how about I give you a nasty little narrative right here in our introduction? A gulp of gossip to get you going?

It will interest you to know, daffy reader, that your narrator was recently invited into a club of sorts, which conducts its business right here on the campus of these medical facilities. While taking my daily stroll through the yard, a very tall and often quiet man came to me with a simple offer: eat the heart of a medium sized animal, and he, along with his organization would welcome me with open arms.

Naturally the first thought to enter my mind was… *What exactly constitutes as medium?*

Certainly the rats on campus would have to fit into the category of small, and the guards' horses are much too large. The more I considered it, the more apparent it became that my recruiter had given me a riddle.

What kind of animal was smaller than a horse, but bigger than a rat? Those were the only beasts living on campus to my knowledge. What could he possibly have meant?

I must confess it took me some time to put the puzzle together, and when I finally figured it out I felt like quite the klutz. It couldn't have been more obvious. If I was to make my way into the fraternity I would need to consume the heart of a man.

As a child I watched my grandfather devour the livers and hearts of raw chickens before preparing his famous gumbo, but I myself have never eaten the innards of any creature, living or dead. Furthermore, I didn't think it likely that any of my fellow inmates would want to donate their blood-muscle for the sake of my initiation, and procuring one by force would prove a steep challenge without access to a decent pair of hands.

I would never accuse the tall quiet man of loving me, or any living creature for that matter. Love is not the way of an organization I wished to join, and if it had been I would have swiftly declined his offer.

Still, there was some inadvertent affection in the task presented. You see, eating the heart of a man is bound to encompass three of my most dearest joys in life. Those being a good challenge, violence, and trying new things.

After realizing what needed to be done, I paced my cell for hours getting down to the bare bones of *how*. My bunkmate did offer his assistance of course, but of all the deplorable things I have ever been, my licentious reader, work-shy has yet to make the list.

No. The contribution I have allowed him is the one that brings you and I together at this very moment. My anonymous accomplice will get his kicks by documenting the execution of my plan in prose. Yes, you've heard right you wicked little word eater. You are about to bear witness to a real live murder. Isn't that fun?

The details of my plan are as follows:

In exactly three minutes, one of the guards on staff will be by with two trays of dinner — one for your narrator, and the other for our trusted transcriber. Today is Tuesday, which means meat paste and gruel are on the menu.

I will not inflict the details of how I managed such a smuggling, but with a pinch of pain and a hint of ingenuity I was able to procure a full sized garden rake from the groundskeeper's quarters. I have already broken off the head of the tool and lodged it into the stump of my left wrist, formerly home to my dominant hand. When dinner arrives I will thrust the staff of the rake through the tray slot in an effort to impale the guard.

Whether or not I am successful in claiming his life at that moment will be of no consequence, for once the deed is done he and his co-workers will undoubtably enter my dwelling in an attempt to punish my deeds.

If you enjoy irony as much as I, you deviant devourer

of draft, then consider this. Were the guard to simply ignore my assault and walk away, he would in all likelihood do so with his life very much still in tact. Moreover, had any of the men responsible for my keeping been attentive enough to prevent me from bringing a sharp, rusty garden tool into my cell, none of their lives would be endangered in the first place.

I do hope that the grand sum of these factors do not escape you. When the official records of today's events are entered into whatever heathenous ledger that such things exist, it will be my madness that carries the weight of causality. But in truth, it is the more nuanced cousins of my disease — both vengeance, and arrogance — possessed by the guards and nurtured through their attendance of this facility, that are the culprits.

And so, blessed bibliophile, you will have to excuse me for repeating myself, but as I stated at the very dawn of this dictation: madness is highly contagious.

Upon entrance of my cell I will rake to death the first man I see, cut out his heart, and eat as much of it as I can before his co-workers can pull me away. I apologize for the lackluster loquacity at this point, but I do believe I hear the guard's footsteps now.

Remember, trite translator, to record only my words, as the guards will be responsible for submitting their own record of todays events.

Yes. That's it. Come on now. Closer... Closer...

I gotcha motherfucker!

Yeah....

Yeah, that worked. He is bleeding good now, isn't he?

Come and get me then you ugly little shitbag! You don't have a clue who you're fucking with!

I hate to speak ill of a soon to be dead man, but you can tell from his language that the boy is rather dense.

Come on then! Come on in here! I'm waiting!

I only bring it up because I do hate to execute a learned man. By the sound of things this fool is far from it.

Oh yeah?! Do it then! I dare you!

All in all this is working out rather well I'd say. Yes. Sounds like they're opening the locks now.

Here's to your enjoyment of my fables rebellious reader. Keep turning those pages, and you'll be hearing from me again soon.

Well hello there guard… You'll do nicely won't you? Get over here you son of a bitch…

THE ORIGIN OF MAN

THERE IS SOMETHING that looks like rock, or skin, or some combination of the two.

Whatever this is…

It is in turbulence — fracturing. Violent tremors the force of a billion earthquakes. Heat that could melt diamonds. Energy that could shape worlds.

Whatever this is…

It is falling. Faster than the speed of light; through a void so vast it seems like a snails pace.

If sound existed, its barrier would be breaking every second. Beaten raw from the sheer ferocity of—

Whatever this is…

It is alive. With a face that screams agony. Eyes gripped with shock, pain, fear, and excitement.

What does it see? Light? Trees? A garden? A love? Fruit forbidden?

Stars.

The void has vanished. The light is dimmed, and now, for

some reason, things exist. Shapes and colors. Forms and movement. An unfolding the likes of which no creature will ever see again.

Matter creates space. Space creates time. Time bleeds the life from…

Whatever this is…

A thing which has been given a destiny. A place made of fire and brimstone. Seas of magma. Clouds of poison. Pure chaos. Endless destruction, and yet somehow, endless potential.

Whatever this is…

It meets its fate with a shattering impact, turning solids into vapor, and darkness to light.

The creature and place are now one.

Destiny. Life. A seed is planted, and from that seed grows the infinite. The magma sinks. The water rises. The poison pushes out to form a sack around this now embryo. Once violent, now fragile.

Whatever this is…

It waits. And the day will come when a name is given onto it by the life it bears. The name will be earth.

The life will be man's.

DA COOLEST NIGGA ON ERF

MY FAVORITE UNCLE once gave me my favorite piece of advice. *Never let 'em see you sweat.'*

It was summertime back when the summers mattered and I had just had my ass kicked by my older cousin — who was also his youngest daughter. I was fighting back tears of rage, champing at the bit for a second round to a fight I felt had been rigged, when just like Jesus on Sundays, Uncle Julius swooped in to press pause on our bullshit.

I counted myself lucky that my father wasn't around. If there was a way to be more embarrassed from getting my lip bloodied by a girl, he'd have sure 'nuff found it and burned it into the pit of my soul.

My uncle's approach was different. To him the fight itself had no meaning. Neither did the infinite possibility of outcomes that could have followed. The only thing that mattered in that moment, or any moment that I can recall being around him, was that the environment orbiting his presence should respect and reciprocate his unwavering cool.

He did not insult my tears, or criticize my behavior, but instead extended an offer for me, to be as cool as he, that never rescinded. He explained that over the course of my life all kinds of things would make me feel all kinds of ways, and it was just fine for this to be the case. But if I ever allowed the things or ways to make me into something less than myself, then the people who witnessed my shame would never forget.

It was just then, somewhere around my eighth trip

around the sun, that the world I knew started to take shape, transporting every window of life to live under a single law. One rule with endless iterations, different folds and twisted roads, but as long as I stayed true I'd never carry the weight of another 'L'.

Or at least that's what I thought.

The bullshit I'm on now started on a Tuesday. I was pushing up Slauson in my 1964 candy orange Chevy Impala — rag top, three-wheel motion — and per usual there wasn't another nigga like me as far as the eye could see. These days my neighborhood was so flooded with transplants and gentrifiers that being plugged in wasn't enough. Somebody had to further the culture. Protect the legacy.

At twenty-three I'd spent a lifetime shaking every hand worth shaking, and gaining access to every back room where politicking got done. All the same I made it a point to let the lames know this wasn't no damn tencil town. South Central Los Angeles was one of the last pockets in coastal America where candor and integrity were more valuable than a dollar bill.

With the game I'd gotten from my uncle, and my cache among the people I was one of the few cats you'd meet that could promise what he wanted and deliver what he'd promised. My presence was a present, but not everybody saw it that way.

Less than four blocks from digging on some Jamaican oxtails I heard the unmistakable sound of a siren's blare. The reds and blues were in my trunk.

I parked out front of some familiar houses when a Latin cop in his mid-thirties strolled up on my ride. Bald head. Tattoos. The type that would've given his left nut for some legit street cred, but hit puberty too late for the Vatos to do anything other than take his lunch money. Guys like him always turned to the PD to make up what they lacked as kids.

"I need you to put your car down on the ground for me", he said, trying his best not to sound inferior.

My driver's side wheel was a good five feet off the pavement, which placed me about a yard over this peon's head. I was sure to let him stew in the reality of mc looking down on him before obliging his request.

"What can I do for you officer?" I said as if he'd just entered my place of business.

"License and registration."

"I got that. Insurance too?"

Pigs hated to see a nigga on top of his shit. From where the cop stood I knew my paperwork had to feel like a hand full of 'fuck you's to his loose authority. I watched him stare about as hard as he could hoping to catch one of those 'fuck you's in black and white. That way he'd have an excuse to jack me up. No such luck.

"Wait here", he told me.

I let him get good and deep in my rearview before floating my next line.

"Say hi to Val for me", I hollered.

"What was that?"

"You're from the Southwest precinct, right? It's 11a.m. That means Valerie Rivers should be on dispatch. Tell her Ty Johnson says hi."

The look on his face was almost worth delaying my Jamaican brunch. I fired up a cigarette and watched him climb in that cramped little wagon of his, then leaned back on my fine stitched leathers, soaking up the California sun like God laid it out just for me.

The stretch of Slauson just east of La Brea was a neighborhood mostly reserved for old folks. The double wide street and narrow sidewalks were a convenience back when they first purchased their drywall bungalows in the sixties and seventies. Back when you could buy a house for fifty-thousand dollars without the sound of fifty thousand cars bleeding through your living room walls every night.

Today the average place on the block carried a million dollar price tag, but even with the increased traffic and crime the natives weren't selling. It'd make me proud to say they didn't want to give whitey the satisfaction of settling on negro land, but the truth was old heads in South Central just weren't the types to go off retiring on tropical beaches. A 'grow where you're planted' sorta thing.

I'd fucked around and caught the thorny side one of those old plants during my run in with the cop.

The heavy slam of her front door led me to believe that Ms. Leonard's nose for other folks' business was in some sort of heat. The stone cold look in her eyes let me know there was more to it. She hadn't thought twice about the pig by the time she'd warbled herself into the passenger's seat of my ride.

"Top of the mornin' Ms. Leonard," I offered with a puff of smoke. "I'm kinda in the middle of something here."

"I need to talk to you," she jabbed.

I did what I could to keep my smile in play for the old woman, but felt my face turning real serious real quick. 'I need to talk to you' was a line I'd expect to hear from the pimps, gangsters, junkies, and street players when they were looking to do a certain brand of business. Who the hell was putting that brand of business on Ms. Leonard's conscience? And why the hell was it looking more and more like Tuesday didn't want to see me and my favorite oxtails be together?

"Do it then," I welcomed.

"Not out here. Inside."

"Yeah, sure. Just as soon as I wrap up—" but she was already out the car and on that Latin boy's ass.

"Excuse me!" She snapped with the full force of her sixty-three years. "Now I know that if you was gonna write a ticket you would've done it while you were sitting in that cockpit. I also know that this boy don't got no kind of warrants or probable cause for you to have him outta the car fuckin' wit' him, so before you get to actin' up like the white boys, just don't. If you from 'round here it's a good chance I know your abuelita, and I'll be sure to tell her exactly what goes on today."

Like I said before, the traffic this side of Slauson was no joke, and a hundred cars whipping through the street next to a man had funny a way of speeding up his decision making. Besides, the guy had already asserted every firm *'Ma'am!'* in his arsenal during Ms. Leonard's lecture, and came up with nothing but an earful. I was quick to chuck a deuce in his direction when he rode out.

"Now what's so urgent you had to put a stream of piss down that cop's leg?"

The inside of Ms. Leonard's home was like something from a catalogue. She had a son out breaking his back on every construction site in town, and he was always good for updating the tiles and fixtures to keep her property at peak value. She took it as a nice gesture, but I always suspected he just didn't want to be caught doing a major remodel after she died.

"I'm drinking", she coaxed. "Care to join me?" Apparently whatever she was after required buttering me up. That was alright.

"Dark if you've got it."

"It's Joanie," She said, dropping three fingers of good whiskey in a coffee mug. "More specifically that nigga she's with."

Joanie was always a serious topic with the people that knew her. She grew up in the neighborhood like the rest of us, but found her way to marrying some white boy Hollywood producer. He pulled her away from all the swinging dicks on the block by promising a life in pictures, but all she ended up with was a five year old Benz and the occasional foot up her ass.

"Look what he's doing to my grand-baby", Ms. Leonard grieved. She showed me pictures of the girl looking all fucked up. Blood in her mouth, eyes swole shut. Serious shit.

"So call the cops." I growled through the whiskey in my throat.

"I did. And it's worse than them not doing anything. Those sick motherfuckers like to see it. One of the bastards told me she should do a better job pleasing her man."

I knew she wasn't lying. Far as I could tell there wasn't a gang on the planet more ruthless than the boys in blue, but the sad fact was a white boy like that was outside my jurisdiction. He had money, connections, and lived in a part of town where niggas like me could get locked up for a bad cough.

I couldn't go saying that out loud of course. My rep was built on making shit happen, and the last thing it needed was the stain of being punked out by an elderly woman.

"Yeah, I see", were the words I finally uttered. "What

kinda solution you looking for?"

"A permanent one," she spit back.

"That's tough. You try making a white body disappear you'll fuck around end up on a Netflix documentary. Especially a white boy like that. The motherfucker's probably got a selfie with Brad Pitt."

"I ain't talkin' about killin' him", she stated keenly.

I kept every eye I had on Ms. Leonard as she limped over to the fireplace and started digging around. I knew she ran tough back in the day, even did a little business with uncle Julius, but sixty-three was sixty-three, and I was wondering just how serious I should be taking our conversation. The shit with Joanie was bad, but for all I knew I was watching this old woman crawl around in search of her lost marbles.

After a minute or so she climbed up carrying a worn leather bag. I was ready to walk out the door watching her struggle to lug it back to the table, but the second she turned it over my better judgement was nowhere to be found.

Green stacks rained down before my eyes, and when the leafy wads finally settled I found myself staring at a hundred thousand dollars in hard cash. It was more than enough to erase my prior concern.

With a *hell the fuck yes* sign clearly written across my forehead, Ms. Leonard slumped down to meet me in my eyes. She wanted to make sure there was no mistaking her request.

"Bring me his fuckin' balls in a jar."

'Never let 'em see you sweat.' The thought ran laps in my brain while Ms. Leonard's leather bag rode shotgun in my Impala.

My first option was to head to the east side, hand the hundred grand to the Eses, and wait for the white boy's balls to arrive at a place of my choosing. In all likelihood this was what Ms. Leonard had in mind when she'd given me the money. She was no stranger to the way things got done around town, and most folks knew the Eses could make just about anything happen for a hundred large.

The problem with that option was it left me on the hook as an unfamiliar middle-man, with no real payoff besides having done a very fucked up good deed for the old lady. The Eses did clean work, but if shit went sideways I didn't expect them or the police to leave me out of it. Even if things went down perfect you never knew when somebody might start looking at you like a loose end.

Option number two was to tap a couple of local guys good for breaking and entering. I could give them the address, plus a twenty band commission for bringing back the jewels. While human castration might not be their area of expertise, taking other people's shit was. If I pitched it right I could get them to see it as an extension of the job.

The B&E angle was a stretch, but it came with an eighty thousand dollar upside, plus the comfort of knowing I was less likely to be ratted out.

I wasn't dumb enough to believe there was a version of this where my life and freedom wouldn't hang in the balance. That ship sailed the second I walked out of Ms. Leonards house with the money. It was clear by now that the only way to survive this thing was by playing it cool. But to come out on top? I was gonna need to be da coolest nigga on erf.

Thursday nights Leimert park transformed into Coachella. A cluster of parked cars blasted music from their trunks while freestyle rappers battled it out all night near 43rd street. Just off of Degnan an African quartet blended electric guitar with steel drums at Ackee Bamboo, while Sonny's Spot and the World Stage offered refuge for any jazz musician with an itch to blow his horn. Old folks like Ms. Leonard could catch a show at the Vision Theater, and the dope dealers held court in a patch of grass across the way.

To be fair, the dope dealers were there seven nights a week, but when Thursdays rolled around they were as much a part of the scene as anybody else. It was a weekly issue where black folks of all prototypes would intersect, which made it the perfect place to order a hit without anyone realizing you'd crossed paths with the hit man.

The band at Sonny's Spot had just laid into a funk thing when I walked through the door. The crimson lights swallowed my mind and body in one gulp, and I slid right to the bar with Ms. Leonard's leather bag on my shoulder.

"Young blood!" Sonny hollered, greeting me with a big hug from across the bar.

"Big Sonny! Thanks for having me, man."

Sonny was always happy to see me. He was good friends with my uncle, and I'd cut my teeth running errands for the two of them as a kid. I knew he wasn't ever hurting for bread so I asked him to hold the cash while I worked out the deal at his place.

My share of the money had already made its home at the safe in my apartment, but twenty thousand dollars was still enough to bait some dummy into risking his life if he got hip to what I was on.

"What you drankin' young blood?"

"Not a damn thing 'til I'm done with this deal."

"Man I don't know how many times I gotta school you, but if you gon' be in this game you betta' know how to do business drunk, high, and witchya dick out. Every kinda terrain, ya' feel me?"

"Yeah I feel you, but go ahead and toss me a water bottle to be sure."

"Haha! Young Blood!"

Sonny handed me some fancy island water and my left foot got to following the electric bass thumping through his speakers. A meeting like the one I was waiting on didn't come with an appointment time, and with Sonny handling the cash I was free to take a load off while I waited.

Sonny was getting good and drunk, digging his own rap about how him and my uncle used to run shit back in the day.

"Man yo' uncle Julius was a motherfucker! Literally. A sister-fucker, a niece-fucker, a side-and-main-bitch-fucker. Ha! Couldn't hit none 'a' my hoes though. My game was too tight."

Sometimes people liked to use me as an excuse to talk to themselves out loud. I thought that was just fine. It left me to work out my own ideas while the other person did all the heavy lifting of having an actual conversation. That's how it went with Ms. Leonard and I ended up eighty racks richer because of it. With any luck I was in for more of the same with the B&E guys.

The cats I'd tapped for the job were a couple of OG's named Chris and Josh. I knew about some young dudes who might have been better suited for the violence, but when it came to getting away clean these two were real professionals. Even if the white boy somehow managed to ruin Ms. Leonard's request, I didn't need to worry about the attempt blowing back on them, and ultimately on me.

The real question was whether or not they'd even take the gig. I put the word out that I'd be at Sonny's Spot with some intel on a place in Beverly Hills, plus an extra twenty large if they could bring me back something special. I was told they didn't mind roughing up home owners, and even did a little bit of killing when the job required, but pinning a man down to cut off his testicles was a tough piece of business. Most guys in the street game understood that even if we lived long enough to get out the life, the memories of what we'd done would never get out of our minds. Niggas that put in the most work were the first to end up living under a bridge or in the nut house.

Still, I knew that if I couldn't convince them to take on the task I'd be on the hook to fork over my eighty thousand to the Eses. Or worse, do the job myself. I didn't want to think about any of that.

When Chris and Josh came through the door I hid my water bottle behind the counter, making sure they saw me take my first and only shot of José. In negotiations like this having the upper hand was always key.

"How we doing tonight fellas?" Sonny shouted.

"Hell, I'd complain but wouldn't nobody give a damn." Chris bellowed back.

"Shit, I know I wouldn't. I want y'all to meet my young bull, Ty."

We all shook hands while Sonny poured the guys drinks. I of course had already reached my limit while waiting. The fact that they showed meant they wanted in on the job, and for wanting my business they'd of course be inclined to match my perceived state of mind. Get on my wavelength, so to speak. I even goated them into extra rounds to ensure my possession of two truth tellers during our conversation.

"We ain't gon' hold you", Chris started out.

The three of us had made our way to a back table where no one would overhear, but Josh had still yet to utter a single word.

"Sonny already vouched for you, so if the place is clean when we ride by we'll do the deed. Just need to know what it is you want brought back."

"His nuts in a jar", I told him. No sense beating around the bush.

"Twenty grand for some food out the kitchen? Shit man, it's yo' money."

"Not those kinda nuts." I watched the two of them carefully to see whose temperature would rise first. Josh didn't budge, but I could tell I'd peaked his interest. Chris on the other hand seemed to have lost a puff of air. He was all business now.

"The home owner you mean?"

"Yeah. He lives with his wife, but I'll make sure she's outta the house when you get there."

"Kids? Pets?"

"Nope." I could feel Chris angling for a way out, but he was too embarrassed to admit it straight up.

"I gotta say", he inched. "This don't really seem like our area of—"

"Why the house?" Josh interrupted. Guess he'd finally found something worth opening his mouth over.

"That's where I know he'll be." I replied. "Plus there'll be shit for you all to steal."

"Twenty thousand dollars worth'a shit?"

"Maybe."

"We don't do jobs in a U-Haul. Twenty thousand' need to be mostly jewelry. Is he a jewelry kinda guy?" Josh was looking to pin me down, but at least he was interested. Unlike Chris, who struggled hard to regain his footing.

"See now if you ain't got the intel…" he revved back up. But it was already too late. Things had started out cool enough, but there was no coming back from me seeing him flinch. I ignored his attempt in favor of the riper prospect.

"I can't make it any clearer what I'm after here," I told Josh. "If you're over there sitting on a professional opinion let's hear it."

Josh pressed his shoulders to the back of his chair. There was an eerie calm about the way he deliberated.

"A professional's opinion…" He let the words hang, unpacking my statement as if it were his own thought. "Well if I go to a man's house and assault him they gonna call that an open and shut case. What we lookin' fo' here is the propa' angle."

I kept it cool. It was obvious that Josh was becoming impressed with himself. All I had to do now was stay the hell out his way and the deal was as good as done.

"Fa' dis to fly you gonna need to catch him slippin'", he finally reasoned.

"Slippin' how?" I asked.

"You after his nuts? My guess he ain't no prince charmin' with the misses. You get him laid up with a bitch? Have her slide somethin' in his drink…?"

"Hold on now, that ain't no fuckin' B&E!" Chris shouted, still desperate to get off a train that had already left its station.

"He won't have a choice but to keep the shit to hisself." I assessed.

"Right you are. Especially if he thinks the girl's got a dick on her."

I cocked an eyebrow. Josh was turning out to be a real devious motherfucker.

"It's a simple con." he went on. "Hire the girl, and have her wear a rubber strap-on. By the time the roophie kicks in he'll swear it's the real thing."

"And that works?" I pressed.

"For gettin' wallets? Yeah. Never tried swipin' a nigga's nuts before."

A dry laugh slipped from the base of my throat, but only to suppress my own discomfort. Something about how casually Josh spoke had me feeling way less in control than I'd expected.

"Right on", I told him. "So unless I missed anything it sounds like we got ourselves a deal."

"We'll get it done this Saturday", he assured. "Somewhere 'round 11pm. Next time we meet you can bring an extra grand for added expenses."

"Money after the fact? I appreciate the trust."

"Trust enough that you still need to deliver to whoever sent you."

"What makes you think somebody sent me?"

"Cuz what the fuck would you want with another man's nuts?"

Never let 'em see you sweat. Dealing with a motherfucker like Josh made it tougher than usual. I left Sonny's Spot with a deal in place, but that guy gave me the heebie jeebies for real.

I gave him and Chris what they'd need to track down Joanie's husband — how he looked, where he worked, what kind of girls he was into. Before we all split Chris made it clear he still wanted a shot at the house. Probably his way of feeling like more than a passenger on the job. I gave him the address, but told him that whatever he did, be sure to leave Joanie out of it.

It occurred to me after the fact that leaving Joanie out

of any of this wasn't much of an option. The future of her marriage had already been decided at that back table in Sonny's spot. Or maybe in her grandmother's kitchen the Tuesday before. The more I thought about it, Ms. Leonard probably had her plan cooked before I was even pulled over outside her house. Not that any of it made a difference. At this point it was what it was, and what it was was just a matter of time.

Still… Joanie. *Damn.*

"Nigga quit hoggin' the joint!"

By the time Saturday rolled around the white boy was just about all I could think of. It was starting to dawn on me that I had set something in motion that would alter the rest of a man's life. Beating women was pretty high on the list of things that lowered my opinion of a guy, but did that really give me the right to take his nuts? Was I breaking my own code by letting the money move me?

For all I knew the weed was fucking with my head. I decided to pass the spliff over to Mike before it could do any more damage.

"My fault homie," I said to no one in particular.

Mike and I were doing our best to keep the front steps of his apartment from flying away. The past few hours had been a steady stream of blunts, beer, cat calls, and bullshit. Mike managed to get a girl upstairs for a few minutes, and we caught a good laugh scaring the shit out of some young

boys on the block. Other than that I hadn't even stood up
to take a piss.

"This shit gettin' old." he told me.

"You got a better play?" I asked.

"I don't know. Sometimes it feels like I could go
anywhere in the world and probably just end up finding
another porch to smoke on. It's only so many thoughts in
your brain, you know? Like one big circle. Can't avoid that
shit."

"Maybe that's how it should be" I offered. "Niggas get
outta pocket, that's when they start to slip."

"But what if this was slippin'? Right here? How would
we even know?"

"Guess we wouldn't", I leveled. "At least not 'til we
got tripped up."

"So you get it then?" he assumed.

"Get what?" I demanded.

This was really the last shit I needed to be hearing. My
vibe was already on life support, and Mike seemed
determined to hold a pillow over its face until the job was
done.

"Nigga, shut up and quit hoggin' the joint", was the
only response I could muster. We laughed, then went back
to watching the block like an old rerun.

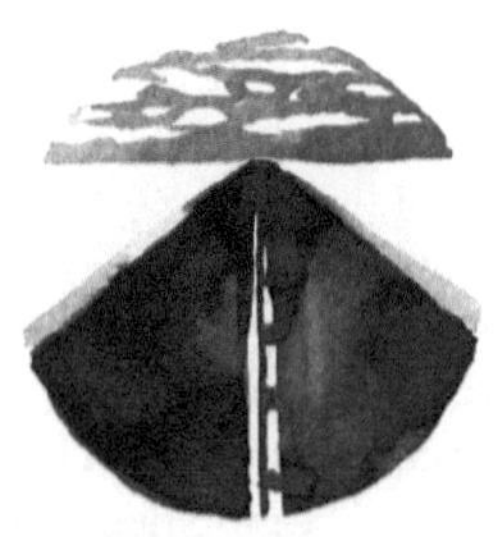

You fucked up…

I knew I should've left that damn joint alone when my thoughts first started to bend. Now I was straight tweaking, walking up and down Crenshaw looking for the end of a run-on sentence in my head.

You fucked up, you fucked up, you fucked up, you fucked up was all I could manage to think. What if a mangled nut sack and rubber dick in his mouth wasn't enough to keep the white boy from telling everything he knew? What if Joanie's house getting robbed left her without a pot to piss in? What if my newfound wealth turned out to be nothing more than bail bond and lawyer fees?

My brain was on fire, but anyone passing me in the street couldn't make out more than a gangster lean and two eyes that clearly read *'not to be fucked with.'*

I might've messed around and roamed the sidewalks like a zombie all night, but was blessed with a pocket of clarity after passing some well-built honeys outside the Taco Drum.

The cure to my condition could be found in a high quality nut, and one Ms. Valery Rivers had been on my mind since Tuesday morning.

"Who is it?" she hollered from somewhere behind the wooden slab.

"Come see."

Val was the kind of girl that would've been a lot prettier had her parents kept her out the streets. There was a heaviness to her brown eyes and scars dotting her chocolate skin. You had to look past the resting anger to see that her face held a soft symmetry worthy of magazine covers. I got a strange satisfaction from feeling like the only one who noticed it.

"Who told you you could show up to my house unannounced?" She said with her head cocked and a hand on her hip.

"You. When you invited me in just now."

"But I didn't invite you in."

"We'll see."

"You're really full of yourself, Ty. You know that?"

"I might've heard it before, sure. But how about if I was just right for once?"

She shot me a look. Little too much emotion in that last line, but it got me inside all the same. I was quick to smile it off.

"You over here makin' a run?" she asked as I closed the door behind us.

"Something like that." I grabbed her by the waist and pressed my hard-on to the back of her jeans. Any other day I'd have set the tone with some witty banter and good laughs, but my slip up at the door only proved that the more I spoke the more likely I was to expose my anxiety.

"So you just gonna get right to it, huh?" In her own way she was pleading for romance. I just didn't have any to offer.

She turned around and I scooped her on my waist, kissing her hard to shut her up. Her curvy frame washed me with a jolt of power that dulled my suffering before I'd even had her clothes off. There was touching, and breathing, and warmth, and movement that reminded me exactly who I was in this world: *Big Ty*. The one and only Mr. *'get it done when you need it done.'* There wasn't a place that I couldn't go. A moment I couldn't conquer.

Visions of the earth laid open at my fingertips, daring me to take what was mine.

Val was on top now, flexing the way she did whenever she came. I flexed back in a rush to join her.

The weed and liquor still had my body, but the nut managed to lift my thoughts to a point of pure wisdom. The hard tingle in my skull and spine took me far beyond the doubt, fear, and second guessing only to see that the recent hell in my mind had been one of my own creation.

The deal with Ms. Leonard was rushed. The combination of her age and sob story knocked me off balance, and the sight of the cash did me in.

Val beckoned me to lay beside her on the floor. My thoughts continued as she rubbed against me.

Joanie was still a wildcard. Would she be grateful? Or forever maimed in the wake of her shotgun divorce?

Then there were the cops. I could count on them to be as useful as a four dollar bill in a crap game when it came to solving crimes. But the only skin in our past games had been black. Heat from a case like this could have me sleeping with one eye open for the next thirty years.

I knew Chris and Josh were famous for evading the law, but they weren't exactly on the same page when it came to this particular job.

There were just too many variables. Too many moving parts for me to go around acting like I had it all under control. It was clear now that the time for keeping shit cool had come and gone. I was knee deep in the part of the game that called for getting my hands dirty.

"Whatever it was that brought you over here I'm glad," Val said as she rubbed a finger on my cheek.

"Yeah? Me too. I'm kinda surprised I didn't hear from you Tuesday."

"What happened Tuesday?"

"When I got pulled over. What? You took the day off or somethin'?"

"No. I was on dispatch, but your name never came

across the radio. Are you sure the cop was from Southwest?"

Hell yeah I was sure. Just as sure as I saw that fucker pressing buttons and moving his lips in the squad car. If he hadn't called dispatch who the hell was he talking to?

A visual of the pig's face when I mentioned Val slapped me right on the brain. At the time I thought I had embarrassed him by pulling his card, but if he was up to some grimy shit I probably tripped up his plan.

"Fuck!" I blurted out.

"What's wrong?" she asked.

Never let 'em see you sweat. "Just some shit I forgot to do. I've gotta hit a corner real quick, baby. I'll call you later."

With every word out my mouth I saw the disappointment creeping onto Val's face. First no foreplay, and now she was stuck holding this sorry excuse instead of the man she'd just made love to. A part of me wanted to tell her the truth, but we both knew that wasn't an option.

I felt her watching as I got dressed. The resting anger back on her brown eyes. I could still see what was behind it, but this time I got no pleasure from knowing what was there. As tough as it was, there was one last thing I needed to know.

"It was 11am when I got stopped. Right over by the gas station on Slauson and La Brea. Can you get me the cop's name?"

I put the top down on my Impala to let the night air slap some sense into me. My game was off kilter in a major way, and from where I sat the root of the problem was that old bitch Ms. Leonard.

"Hello?" she quivered over the line.

I wanted to reach through the phone and slap that sweet cookie baking grandma routine right out of her throat, but it was too soon to be showing my hand.

"It's me." I said coldly.

"Is it done?" she asked.

"It will be, but I need you to get Joanie outta the house right now. Tell her to come see you so you can have eyes on her. And call me when you do."

I hung up the phone feeling dangerous like a motherfucker, and hoped for her sake that Ms. Leonard wasn't dumb enough to try and play me.

Uncle Julius was on my mind as I lifted the throwaway .40 cal from my belt. I knew I'd have to apply pressure to get the truth from Ms. Leonard, and my pockets held a few extra clips in case Chris and Josh got disagreeable about calling off the hit. It also hadn't escaped me that I may need to snuff a cop depending on his level of involvement.

The shit was crucial, but for the first time since Tuesday there was nothing on the horizon that could bait me into breaking a sweat. Tonight that burden was reserved for the pig, Ms. Leonard, Chris, Josh, and whoever else found themselves staring down the barrel of my heat.

A bug flew in and out of my ear. The cold bit my face as wet grass doused the ankles of my socks and my knees began to sore from thirty plus minutes of squatting.

At 8:46pm Ms. Leonard returned my call a to confirm Joanie's arrival, and before 8:47 the heel of my boot was kicking in her back door.

The two of them screamed as I gripped my pistol, stepping into the kitchen from outside. I knew the element of surprise would hasten my journey to the truth, and the wave of information broke just as soon as I set foot on that living room rug.

"Joanie?" I snapped. "You motherfucker! You in on this shit too?"

That lying whore's face was as smooth as a baby's leg. My eyes narrowed in search of so much as an ill-popped pimple, but found nothing more than overpriced make-up and a botoxed brow. Of course the picture Ms. Leonard showed me Tuesday had been a fake.

"Ty, please! Please don't kill me!" Joanie pled.

I could already see the water welling her eyes as she held a shaky finger to her grandmother. "She made me do it. It was all her idea!"

Ms. Leonard hopped up in a hurry to feed Joanie the back of her hand.

"Bitch quit beggin'! We don't owe this nigga, or that jiggalo motherfucker Julius a gat' damn thang."

I sent a bullet whistling through the television to refocus their attention. As much as it pained me to break up a knife fight between two backstabbers, my schedule didn't permit me taking in a show.

"Damnit!" Ms. Leonard exclaimed. "I just got that tv!"

"And I just got these motherfuckin' bullets. Now sit your ass down before I get my money's worth."

I'd seen the look of a nigga ready to die more than once in my life. It was hard to believe this crazy ass sixty-three year old would be standing in front of me with that same white hot rage.

What the hell was her problem? Before getting pulled over I couldn't remember us exchanging more than some small talk in passing, and here she was ready to risk it all over a four day old beef? The fucked up part was that if I killed her, I was gonna have to end Joanie too. I pressed the tip of my gun to her grand-baby's head to be sure she knew the rules.

"This what you want?" I asked without ever taking my eyes off the old woman.

Her glare softened. Joanie's pitiful sobs were turning out to be the key to her grandmother's sanity, which was good to know. There was no reasoning with a person who had nothing to lose. Visions of me burying the two of them out back began to fade once she landed her wrinkled behind back on the loveseat.

"I know it was you stuck that cop on me. How long you been plannin' this shit?"

"Yo' whole damn life", she growled.

"Don't fuck with me", I barked. "You know I'm connected everywhere, right? Your son's wife still go to to church with Pastor Evans? Over there on 56th? Maybe after I'm done with Joanie's husband I can do her next? Maybe I kill all your in-laws, then your grandkids, then your kids, then your last livin' sister, Debrah?"

As coldhearted as she might have been I knew I'd found a soft spot with Ms. Leonards family. Her stone wall facade couldn't hide what her silence was already telling me. I was finally about to get some answers.

"How much does the cop know?"

"He don't know nothin'," she snorted. "It's like I said, he's from here and I'm good with his granny. I needed you to feel like you owed me for what I was askin' so I called in the favor."

"Bitch you've gotta be joking. You tellin' me you' out here runnin' some kinda senior citizens mafia?"

"I'm tellin' you I didn't tell neither one of them shit.

This is between the four of us. Nobody else."

"Nah, you mean the three of y'all. You pulled all them stops just to mix me up in your beef with the white boy. Well fuck all that. I'm out."

A creepy little smirk etched the bottom half of Ms. Leonard's face. She shook her head.

"Julius keep' you closer than his own sons but still won't tell you no more than he would a two-dollar hoe. I ain't talkin' about Joanie's husband you dumb shit. That uncle of yours stuck' his dick in everything wasn't nailed down. Includin' my daughter!

"So?" I poked. "You jealous?"

"So that's your cousin you're holdin' a gun to, fool!"

And there it was. My cousin. His daughter. For a split second I was eight years old all over again. After all this uncle Julius was the last piece of the puzzle, but this time he wasn't here to press pause on my bullshit. This time the world was orbiting *my* energy, and it wasn't tears I was holding back, but a clip full of copper headed death pellets for whoever thought I was the one to play with.

"Puttin' his favorite child in my pocket seemed the best way to get him thinkin' on the one he left behind", Ms. Leonard bragged. She thought she was morphing into some sort of supervillain.

"That true?" I asked Joanie.

"I don't know", she struggled. "Maybe. He used to visit when I was little. I called him daddy. He call me sweet girl. But then my gran-gran made him so mad. The two of them argued one day and that was the last time I saw him."

"How sore a loser you gotta be to abandon your own daughter? The nigga owed me money so I took it."

Ms. Leonard had no shame when it came to twisting the knife in Joanies childhood wound. "Joanie'd never've married that wife beating son-of-a-bitch if Julius was where he needed to be. Or even stepped in to set the bastard straight."

"Don't look like she gettin' beat to me."

"Cuz a woman got to be dead and buried 'fore she get so much as a tear shed for her. If I didn't fake that picture nobody'd wanna believe anything was goin' on. But I did fake it, and now he's gonna know we mean business about nullifying the prenup. After everything him and Julius put her through, the two of them's gonna make Joanie a rich woman."

I threw my head back and let out the biggest belly laugh of my life. I hadn't been caught slipping. There was no grand conspiracy happening behind my back. All I had done was step my foot into a pile of sucka' shit left behind by none other than my beloved uncle.

It was finally starting to dawn on me that not only had I surpassed the need for childhood advice, I surpassed the man who'd given it to me. Hell, even the pig was turning out to be nothing more than an errand boy.

I continued to cackle at the sight of poor Joanie still trapped in her grandmother's clutches. The generations before us had grown inefficient, and she, unlike me, had allowed herself to become its ration. Maybe there should have been sympathy in my heart, but all I could feel was the unbridled joys of freedom, and a stab of deep hatred for anyone threatening to take it away.

"Oh man!" I let out in an effort to subdue my heavy heaving. "So you stole from my uncle. And somehow still lived to be sixty three years old? You ever think that might mean he was givin' you the money? Then spent the last however many years away from his own daughter just to avoid killin' her gran-gran?" My head shook with genuine disappointment. "I had a feelin' you might be crazy, but stupid too?"

"You gon' get enough disrespectin' me in my house, nigga. I wasn't too dumb to play you like boo-boo the fool now was I?"

She did have a point. It also reminded me that the clock was running down on the white boy, and as fun as all this had been there were much bigger fish be battered and dipped.

"Sho' ya' right Ms. Leonard. And after hearing that speech of yours I even agree with you a little. Joanie does deserve her piece of the white boy's pie. Lucky for her I'm a true believer in reparations. I'll make sure he does the right thing. He's gonna keep his nuts though. Just like I'm keepin' that money you gave me for the job."

I let some seconds pass to see if she was dumb enough to oppose the best possible outcome of having a gun-toting killer in her living room. Fortunately her only response was shit-eating silence.

"Glad we agree", I went on. "Now it's just two things we need to get out the way before I split. Number one…" I refocused the .40 between Joanie's eyes. "… and I can't stress the importance of honesty enough here. Where can I find your husband?"

"The Savoy" she piped without hesitation.

"Good girl." My trigger hand drifted over to Ms. Leonard. "And you? Well I think you owe me an apology."

I could've fried eggs on that old lady's forehead when the words 'I'm sorry' finally dripped from her tongue. I was dead serious about killing her and Joanie when I first arrived, but once I had the situation in hand it was all theatrics. Hurting chicks had never been my bag, and I definitely wasn't about to go killing customers over uncle

Julius' malfunction. It wouldn't surprise me in the least to find out he had a dozen Joanies running around LA, and I was too busy keeping my game tight to be cleaning up another man's mess.

"Turn around for me please."

The bouncer outside the Savoy patted me down while I fired up a KOOL. I left the .40 cal in my Impala in hopes of pulling off a lighter touch on Chris and Josh, who were bound to grow itchy trigger fingers at the sight of me crashing the hit. In dealings like ours a twenty thousand dollar cash payment was as good as a blood oath. Sidestepping the protocols of such an arrangement at the moment they'd be most exposed was going to invite some understandable distrust, and the inevitable appetite for a trusty solution.

The good news was I didn't need to worry about them drawing down in a club full of witnesses. I'd get the chance to explain that there was no police wire on my person, nor plans of a double cross on my mind. Best case scenario they'd take me at my word. I could pay off my thousand dollar tab and send the two of them home with smiles on their faces.

The more likely outcome however would be that they didn't buy a single thing I had to say, and I'd wind up having to body one or both of them somewhere up the block. In that case I couldn't risk being caught with the murder weapon at the front door.

"You good", the bouncer ordained "but it's no smoking inside."

"Whatever nigga", I pressed, blowing a cloud of poison right in his fat face. There was a standing invitation for him to try and stop me as I passed by with the Kool still on my lips. He was a wise man to turn down the fade.

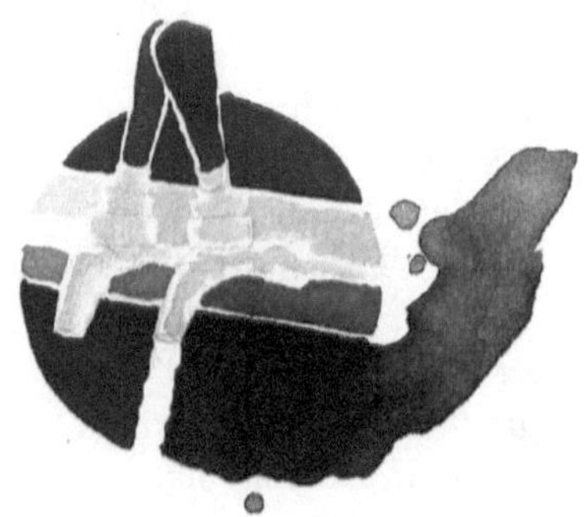

Walking in that box of heavy bass and humidity felt like catching a contact high. Long tube blacklights scaled the top wall of the room, supplying every creature in attendance with a personalized neon glow.

In the moment I could picture myself overlooking a flock of undressed souls. As if some cosmic vision had laid bare any fear or insecurity that might work to my advantage.

All around me were women desperate to conceal their every flaw, and men eager to be relieved of their hard earned pussy-bait.

It was suddenly clear how Sonny could be so lax in the execution of his hustle. Joints like this were an absolute goldmine, and a player's only task would be not to interrupt the fools as they cast away their loot.

The deeper my thoughts ran the more my shit show of a night had me weighing the prospect of a new career, and I began to wonder if eighty thousand dollars could meet the market value of an effective reset button.

In the midst of my calculations I spotted the white boy curled up with some fine piece of chocolate on a corner booth. I put a pin in my daydream to try and figure whether the girl was in on my con, or running her own.

Chris and Josh were nowhere to be found, which would make the honeypot my one and only vehicle for contact. Problem was it looked like I'd need to pry her from the cold dead fingers of Joanie's husband just to get a word in.

"Lemme get a club soda", I told the bartender. The woman behind the counter shot me a condescending look.

"Seven Dollars", she demanded, releasing the fuzzy liquid from its tap. I peeled a hundred dollar bill from my pocket knot and dangled it just out of her reach.

"You can keep the change", I teased. "But I need you to do me a favor." She perked right up.

"What d'ya need?"

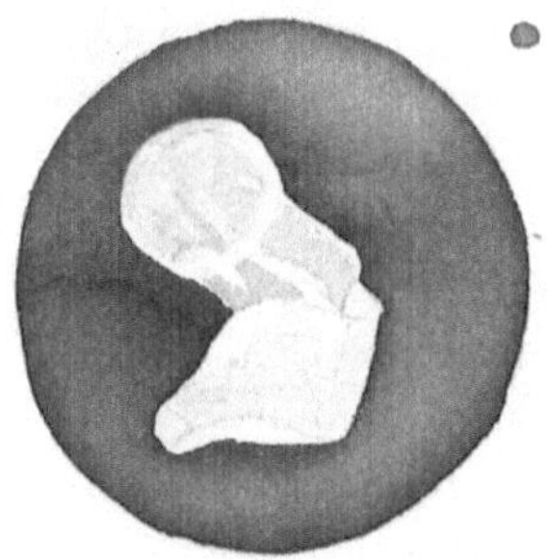

Joanie's husband was making the absolute most of his conquest — coming up with excuses to put his hands on her hair, face, arm, and breast in rapid succession. I was almost impressed by the nonchalant manner in which he went about molesting the girl in such a public space. With any luck he'd run his grubby fingers across the rubber dick Josh mentioned and the whole hit could be over before it started.

Unfortunately the clock was pulling up on 10:40 and I didn't have time to see if the hypothetical would become a reality.

I chopped a finger through the air, signaling for the barkeep to make her way to the booth. I stood from my wooden stool and made way in the opposite direction.

If the girl was in fact working for Chris and Josh my hope was that she'd believe the barkeep's message was from one of them, or at least get spooked enough to come and see who was hip to her game.

But after several minutes of looking like an absolute creep hovered outside the bathrooms, and the non-proverbial cut off still fast approaching, I realized how wrong I was.

My thoughts shifted to walking out there and breaking up the two lovebirds by hand. It was a move that would all but guarantee my death duel with the contractors, not to mention implicate me to Joanie's husband. I had to wonder if either outcome wouldn't be more manageable than the blowback of castrating a rich white man.

I took a half step toward the main hall of the club when something cold and sharp grabbed me by the ribs. I turned and found a none to pleased Chris on the controlling end of an eight inch blade.

"Good to see ya' brotha''', I floated.

"You s'posed to be waitin' to hear back from us", he hissed.

"Change of plans. We need to talk."

"Talk, huh? I'on' 'member tellin' you where the shit was goin' down. Maybe you an' the white boy been talkin' this whole time?" He ran his hand up my shirt in search of a wire.

"C'mon bro. You really think—"

"I ain'cha bro! And don't tell me what to think. Na' gimme one reason I'on' open you up and flush yo' insides down one of these toilets."

"Cuz I realized you was right. Back at Sonny's Spot? This ain't the move, man. I came here to call the shit off." I could feel the knife pinch as Chris applied more pressure. He wasn't buying it.

"If I was right then that means I'm right now. You been playin' us from day one. Only thing I ain't figured is if ya' boy out there is a police. But I don't need you to tell me. I don't need you for shit."

"Well I do still owe you that g-ball."

"And we gon' settle up right now." With the knife still at my ribs I was guided through the thick of the club.

Over a sea of sweaty bodies I saw the chocolate drop leading Joanie's husband to the front door. There was nothing I could do to stop them.

"Believe you me Josh is gonna have a good time carvin' ya' boy up. I'll give him ya' best when I'm back at the motel."

"He ain't my boy", I tried to reason.

"But here you is dyin' to save his ass. *Tsk, tsk.* Sad story."

It felt like an eternity by the time we reached the rear exit of the building. I opened the door to find a vacant alley littered with cigarette butts and battle worn prophylactics. Chris was surely planning to leave me dead in this place.

As soon as I felt the metal door shut behind us I backed an elbow into his jaw. He stumbled but not before piercing the flesh of my upper hip. I sucked in a deep breath to counter the rush of pain as he charged again.

"You motherfucker!" he shouted with another swipe of the blade. But this time I was quick enough to sidestep his attack. With fleeting strength I plucked his arm from the air. The momentum allowed me to pull him off balance while I launched a hail Mary of a headbutt. I felt his nose bend and crack against the top of my skull.

"Gat' damnit!" he cried out. Clinks of the knife echoed the alley as it skipped away from the two of us. Chris landed on the ground just after me, and leaking just as much blood.

I heard the shuffles before witnessing him make it up to his hands and knees. I managed to lift myself for a moment in response, but the pain quickly pulled me back to the pavement. Soon enough the shank was restored to his possession.

"The fuck kinda nigga goes lookin' to buy a gat'damn lynchin'!" He yelled.

"I came to call the shit off dummy!"

"Bullshit!" Chris seemed to fly across the alley as he lunged in my direction. Fortunately he landed wide right with the tip of his blade chipping against the asphalt. I could see now that his eyes were filled with blood.

He tried to wipe them clean but the gravel and dirt on his hands only made matters worse.

"What is it then, huh? You a cop or a snitch?" He was fishing. A dangerous game of Marco Polo mixed with Russian Roulette. He crouched low with the weapon in striking position. I kept my mouth shut.

With the help of a second wind I rose to my feet, creeping around in search of an angle to attack. But the wound on my side was making me sluggish and the sound of my steps triggered him to fling the blade in all directions.

I lifted a piece of wood from the ground and held still.

"C'mon wit yo' bitch ass! Come and get it!" he challenged.

He angled himself to take a stab at me. When the moment was right I tossed the wood to his opposite side. As if his eyes still worked he snapped his head in that direction and I immediately pounced, grabbing his wrist in an effort to claim the knife. We struggled.

"You stupid fuck!" I told him. "The white boy is connected. You gotta call the shit off."

"Connected to who?"

"Brad Pitt motherfucker!"

He released a hand to claw at my face. It was all I needed to overpower his grip on the handle. I twisted the tip of the blade back toward him while he used the last of his strength to prevent me from digging that dirt out of his eye my damn self.

"Where they goin'? Huh? You said motel. Gimmie a name."

"Fuck you!" He yelled, still battling to keep the blade at bay.

'*Fuck me?*' I thought. This guy was fumbling what could have been a smooth getaway, and had the nerve to curse me? I lost my shit.

"You soft, you know that? I knew it the day I met you. I can always tell a scared nigga. Now yo' dumb ass is 'bout to die in this fuckin' alley."

"Go ahead", he bucked. "Josh'll kill you next. I've been tryna keep that crazy motherfucker in check for years. Then here you come settin' him off. You deserve everything comin' yo' way. You ain't got a clue who he—"

But Chris never finished the sentence. His strength had failed him, and the knife was now handle deep in the base of his throat. I didn't mind one bit watching him drown in his own blood. Piss puddled his pants while his life dwindled to an involuntary twitch of the foot.

I made quick work of probing his remains. He may not have been willing to confess what my next move should be, but that didn't mean the answer wasn't somewhere on his person. I soon came across a two by four inch business card in the slip of his wallet. On it was the name of a familiar motel: *'The Bougie Squirrel Motor Inn'*

I reached into my pocket and lit up two cigarettes. One for me, and the other to pack between the lips of my now-dead contractor. In both cases it was only a matter of pageantry. Each of us was too numb for the nicotine to bring any real relief.

I buried his wallet back in the same pocket I found it, along with what was left of my pack of Kools. A parting gift of sorts.

It took a while for the lighter's flame to take possession of Chris' shirt collar. Once it did I wiped the BIC clean and placed it in his palm, wrapping his fingers around for good measure.

The blaze was rising, and the flames chewed through his skin as I drug his body over the mess of blood I'd leaked by the door. It was all I could think of to cover my tracks. Nothing guaranteed that any of this would be enough to fool the cops, but I had to try. With a hand pressed to my hip wound I forced myself down the alley to the nearest backstreet, leaving Chris to waste away under the glow of fire.

By the time I reached my Impala I could hear the rise

of terrified screams back at the club. Bodies rushed outside while the shrill of the fire alarm echoed the block.

There was blood on my seat — mine, Chris', I couldn't tell. I felt it drip as I probed for the fifth of Henny underneath, and the flap of my open wound creased up against itself.

The bottle I found was warm, but it didn't matter. With a pop of the cork I threw my head back to swallow three big gulps, then poured what was left over my torn flesh. My pain doubled over. It was hard to know whether the liquor was killing bacteria or crippling my cells the way it did when I drank.

I reached over to the glove box and unhooked the latch. Inside was a stockpile of gauze and sutures for moments like this. As I dressed the wound my phone began to ring.

"You okay baby?" The voice on the line asked. It was Val.

"Copacetic", I replied. "What's up?"

"Are people screaming? Wherever you are sounds terrible."

I had forgotten all about the mayhem at the club. Tuned it out. Val reminded me I needed to get far away from where I was at, and with the quickness.

"I don't hear anything", I lied as I drove out into traffic. The less Val knew the better.

"I got the name of the guy who pulled you over." She told me. "Officer Thomas Diaz. I can give you the rest of his information if you wanna write it down?"

There would be no need for a pen and paper. I knew nothing about the night would escape my memory any time soon. "Shoot", I told her. "I'll remember."

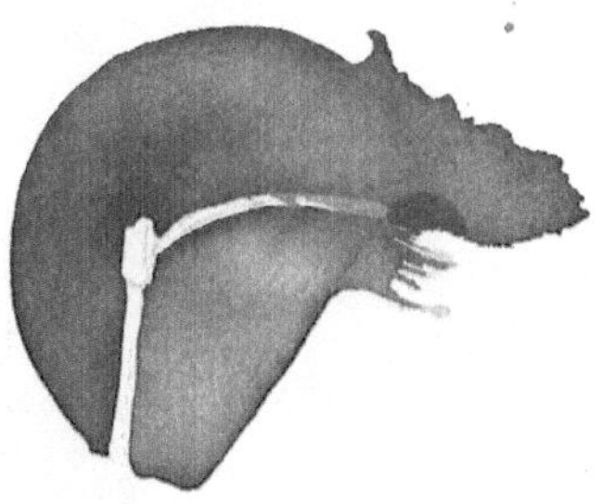

City lights pulsed like a manic heartbeat over my windshield. The hydraulics had my car rocking like a boat in a storm as I swung in and out of every southbound lane I could find.

If I was lucky, the fire back at the club had gotten too big for anyone to use the alley as a means of escape. Chris would be allowed to cook through and through while traces of my DNA grew as inconsequential as the spit, sperm, piss, shit, coochie juice, and whatever the hell else lived back there before it. By the time the cops arrived all they'd find was some drunken fool too wasted to light his own cigarette. That was of course if I got very lucky.

Dangling from the hem on that glib cloak of fortune was one loose thread in the shape of two white testicles. Unless I hauled ass to the motel my hopes of escaping this mess would surely unravel. There would be a direct line drawn from Chris' body, to the white boy's balls, back to me. The barkeep would remember the message I gave. The bouncer may or may not recall my brand of smokes if pressed. I put the peddle to the floor.

I couldn't help but think how much of a fool Chris had been back at the club. All he had to do was listen. I knew showing up to the hit unannounced would rub him and Josh the wrong way, but to not even hear me out? Even if I was working with the white boy, wouldn't it be in his best interest to find out everything he could? And Josh. What was Chris trying to tell me about him? I guess I'd be finding out soon enough.

My wound was wrapped and dry by the time I reached the motel parking lot. The .40 clip was nice and full, with a cherry topper ready to go in the chamber. I gripped its handle with both hands, creeping low and moving fast as I put distance between myself and the Impala. In my mind there was still time to stop the hit.

I knew there would be no need to finesse my way past the lodge attendant. The beauty of a place like the Bougie Squirrel was that nobody asked and nobody told. I watched the whores out front turn their heads like flamingos at the sight of my weapon, which I was brandishing with no shame.

As I moved toward the building's main structure I could feel my soul sink to the pavement. The deep whirl of the many air blowers made the ground shiver beneath my feet, and the vibrations coursed all the way up to my knees. It was as if the motel was imposing on me the very nerves I tried so hard to suppress. It had already been one of the longest nights my life, and somehow my entire future still rested on what came next.

I knew that without the benefit of x-ray vision, finding Josh and the white boy was gonna be a tall order. So what? I had do what I was here for.

I came to the first in a long line of numbered doors on the first level walkway. I held my face up to the adjacent window and cupped one hand above my eyes hoping to see inside, but the curtains were thick, and shut too tight for me to see anything. The only thing I could make out were the convincing moans of a woman in heat.

I did my best to let those passionate cries soothe my thoughts. To believe that Joanie's husband was in there making good use of the Honeypot. It would mean I had beaten Josh to the punch, and could get the drop on him before he did any unnecessary damage.

But as much as I wanted it to be true, the belief never set in. My gut had already staged mutiny against my intelligent mind, and braced itself for the absolute worse.

I proceeded to make my way down the dim lit corridor. The air was unusually chill for an LA night.

Using my only available spy gear — my eyes, ears, and instincts — I set out to determine which door might be the one to boot down. I was able to detect much more love making, drug dealing, partying, and and other standard motel activity, but not Joanie's husband.

As I neared the end of the row an unmistakable sign swam through the night air. A voice, whispering. Singing a song that felt like the soundtrack to my life. The clearer it became, the harder it was to believe.

Curtis Mayfield's Little Child Runnin' Wild was beckoning from the very last door in the row. His wails were seductive, yet chilling at the same time.

When I approached the room I noticed that the golden latch had been propped between the door frame, allowing access for anyone who wanted to enter. *He couldn't have been expecting me. Could he?*

I pressed the door open, slowly, with the .40 propped in firing position. I took a smooth and deep breath in preparation for whatever I might find on the other side, but nothing could prepare me for what my eyes took in.

Josh was here, dancing happily to the music that gave

away his location. Deep in the throes of a Chi Town two step.

A marijuana blunt swung from his lips as he sang along with Curtis. A red hot clothing iron was clutched in his right hand, which limited his dance to the length of its cord plugged in a nearby wall.

Lying on the bed beside him like some ritual sacrifice was Joanie's husband. The white boy was unconscious, with his back on the bed and his bare feet touching the floor. His knees were spread far apart and he was completely naked from the waist down. A river of blood had formed on the plastic sheet that lined the bed and carpet. The operation was still in progress.

With an unfathomably smooth piece of motion, Josh transitioned out of his two-step to hunch over the white boy's body, still dancing with his hips head and shoulders.

Using the index and thumb of his free hand, he lifted the flaccid penis of Joanie's husband, then pressed the hot iron onto the gaping lacerate that once carried his ballsack. The white boy's skin hissed from the heat, and with a twisted smirk, Josh turned to face me.

"Thirty — Five — Minutes", he said with the calm tone of a radio DJ.

"What?" I buckled. I was fighting back the hot bile that rushed to my throat. If not to save me from the shame of a weak stomach, to prevent the spread of any evidence that I was ever in the room. At least making myself hard to track was something I could still do. When it came to saving Joanie's husband, I was already too late.

"You wonderin' how close you got to stoppin' me." He turned back to his business and and removed the iron to see if the wound had been well enough sealed. Then carefully laid the white boy's penis onto his stomach so it would't touch the mending skin. He rose to his feet.

"Thirty-five minutes." I knew he was looking to get in my head.

"How'd you know I'd come?" I laid out.

"I had a feelin'", he said.

He set the iron down on a nearby table and picked up a mason jar containing an unmistakable pair of testicles. A mixture of blood and pickle juice keeping them afloat.

"This was really a terrible idea", he went on. "You'd have been a fool not to see it at some point."

"If it was a terrible idea then why'd you go through with it?"

"Didn't Chris tell you? Cuz I'm a terrible person." He was standing directly in front of me now. Offering to hand over the jar containing what I had paid for. I didn't budge.

The .40 was in perfect position to take Josh's head off his shoulders. I wondered why I hadn't already pulled the trigger and gotten it over with, just as I wondered how he could be so blasé about everything happening in this room.

"Guess Christopher won't be joinin' us, huh?"

"Motherfucker tried to kill me." I said.

"So you killed him? Good for you."

"Don't try to play me, nigga. Go sit your ass down."

I watched him stare at me for a few seconds before jerking his body into a Bo Jangles slave nigga tap-dance. A dance that he continued as he made his way to the only chair in the room.

His energy shifted with the sharpness of an edge thin razor as he calmly lowered his body onto the metal seat. I had still yet to make up my mind as to exactly what brand of crazy this nigga was, but whatever his disease it didn't prevent him from exercising an impressive level of personal control. He was almost presidential in the way he looked at me.

"So", he started as if beckoning a tour guide. "What now? You gon' kill me?"

"Hell yeah I'm killin' yo' crazy ass." I fired back.

"Yeah? And uh…" He pointed to Joanie's husband with a thumb, covering his mouth as if someone might overhear. "What about him?"

"Him?" I breathed calmly, finally slipping back into

my element. "He's pullin' the trigger."

The look on Josh's face made me believe he was genuinely impressed.

"Yeah. I see it", he said grandly. "Wrap his hand 'round the gun. Fire it off until I'm dead, and when the cops come, won't be no case left to solve."

At this point I was done with the mind games. I refused him the satisfaction of a response as I stepped carefully over toward the bed, fully prepared to execute the plan he so astutely spelled out.

Before I made it to the white boy's side Josh opened his mouth again.

"And I'm guessin' you already picked up the ledger? Makin' sure nobody don't read ya' name?"

I stopped cold. This motherfucker just would not stop.

"The fuck you talkin' bout now?" I said.

"Oh? Christopher ain't tell you? I keep a book on every nigga I do bidness wit'. For accountin' purposes. I still got you penned in for that g-ball, ya know?"

Was he bluffing? It was getting harder and harder to tell which way was up with this fool. My eyes mulled over the latex gloves on his hands. The thick plastic he'd laid out to prevent the spread of DNA evidence. And the surgical precision of the white boy's wound. Everything was very clean, and exact. I couldn't put it past him to have a book of records somewhere with my name on it.

I also couldn't picture going through the labor of escorting him back to his house. Definitely not at the risk of leaving things untied there in the motel. The longer I stayed in the middle of things, the more likely I was to implicate myself in whatever piece of tonights puzzle the cops managed to pick up on.

I also couldn't afford to cut him loose. Josh was clearly dangerous, and I was starting to grasp the meaning behind Chris' last words.

"Iv'e been holding that crazy motherfucker back for years, and here you come settin' him off..."

I had awakened a monster and murdered his keeper all in the same night. There was no telling what he would do if I allowed him to go free.

My mind was racing. And the longer I took to respond to his threat, the more control I was handing over.

Think, Ty. Think!

All at once the play took shape in my head. I still had an ace in the hole. One that could take this whole night off of my conscience, leaving me with my rep, freedom, and bankroll fully intact.

Josh's game was clear to me now as well. I lowered my gun in an attempt to match his ease.

"You a smart man, Josh."

He frowned at the sound of his own name.

"Let's say I leave you here", I went on. "Alive. What's your next play?"

"I already done the job. You take yo' trophy over there…" He was pointing to the jar of testicles. "… I clean up this mess. We both get on wit' life. Done deal far as I see it."

"What about ya' boy Chris? I'm s'posed to believe you not gonna come lookin' for no get-back over him?"

He smiled at me the way grown ups do a child asking for candy.

"I think you can tell by now…" he replied. "Christopher was holdin' me back."

In a way I knew that to be the truth, but it wasn't really an answer to my question about the get-back. I made the decision to leave it be. With the play I'd hatched none of it mattered anyway. Josh was gonna do me the favor of cleaning up this mess, and by the morning I'd have his ass nailed to a fucking wall.

"Aight then. Sounds like our deal is done. Let's say you take that rack I owe you out of your partner's share."

"Tha's aight wit me", he buttoned.

I watched him lift the jar from the table one last time. He took a moment to look it over, admiring his work.

"This really was a terrible idea", he added as he placed the jar in my hand.

As I replayed our exchange I realized just how many things Josh was right about. Not the least of which being that this had all been a terrible idea.

But he was also right in the way he played things. I could've killed him at any point back at the Bougie Squirrel. The only reason I didn't was because of how cool he kept it. There were moments when I actually believed he wanted to die.

A combination of adrenaline and fatigue had me unable to revel in any pain from my wound. There was one last step to take before I could put this night to bed. My ace in the hole. A get out of jail free card somewhere on the other side of the fancy mahogany door before which I stood.

I knocked hard with the butt of my gun.

"Come on now!" I shouted. " I ain't got all night.

The porch light snapped on. The door swung open, and I met my host with a toothy smile. A gush of shock and anger ran from his face, but I knew it was something he'd have no choice but to get over.

"Officer Diaz", I said warmly. "Remember me?"

A woman's voice hollered from somewhere inside the

house. "Who's that, honey?"

"Work stuff", he answered hastily. "Go back to bed." The lie flowed like butter from his lips. Before the woman had a chance to respond the front door was shut behind him, and the palm of his hand was shoving me out of view of the house windows.

"How the fuck do you know where I live, shitbag?"

The two of us became engulfed by the deep shadows of the night. Somewhere between the house and its two car garage.

Knowing that we were out of sight I slapped his arm away and shoved the .40 nozzle into his chest.

"You kiss your granny with that mouth?" I taunted. "How she doin' by the way?"

A vein the size of a pinky finger bulged from his neck, and blood vessels cracked a bright red under his skin. He was pissed. That was good.

"Come on now Tommy. Who you really mad at here, huh? I was mindin' my own business when you decided to come fuckin' with me."

"I didn't even write the God damn ticket!" He spoke with a sharp whisper. "And now you're showing up to my house? That's a bad move, homeboy."

"Oh I'd say it's the perfect move officer Tommy. You right about one thing though. You and me is definitely homeboys now."

"Fuck you."

"Do you know why your granny had you stop me that day? It was so her friend could hire me to cut a niggas nuts off."

His brow furrowed. His anger forced to make room for confusion.

I pulled the jar with the white boy's balls out of my coat's inner pocket and held it up for him to see. His eyes grew wide with horror.

"Don't run from it Tommy. 'Homeboy'. See you and me is what they call accomplices. I know you know that word, right?”

“No”, he pled.

“Oh yeah. And as your accomplice I’m here to explain how you can make good on the bullshit you put us in.”

I could tell he wanted to run. His eyes darted back and forth from my face to the pistol pressed between his ribs. He’d probably been trying to remember whatever move they taught him back in the academy to disarm a potential threat, but it was obvious he didn’t have the guts to try it. The fight faded from his face as he resigned himself to hearing me out.

“What do you want?” He asked regretfully.

“For you to do your job. Make sure this here crime gets pinned on the motherfucker that did it.”

“Isn’t that you?” He pride with every ounce of boldness he had left.

“Nigga do I look like a fuckin’ psychopath? I outsourced the job. Now all you gotta do is solve the crime, be a big hero, and make sure none of it blows back on you, or your accomplice. Sound like a plan?”

He was nodding his head before I even finished talking. I knew I had the motherfucker in check.

“Ye- Yeah”, he stammered. “Yeah, okay. Easy. Just tell me who the guy is and I’ll get it done.”

“See that?” I watched him gag as I handed him the jar. “I knew you could do it homeboy. Now the guy you need to pick up’s name is Jos—“

PIFF!

I hadn’t finished my sentence before the blood splattered across my face. The pigs body fell to the ground with his head exploded off of its shoulders.

PIFF!

Before I could make sense of what had happened a hole burned through my leg and I fell down beside him. I saw his dismembered face next to the white boys testicles and a broken jar.

I looked up and found myself staring into a six inch

silencer, screwed to the end of a long nose desert eagle. It took a few seconds to make out the face behind the trigger, but once I realized who it was I was washed with regret.

'Never let 'em see you sweat.'

"Josh", I said trying not to betray my panic. What the fuck are you doin' man?"

"Ya' know I really did think about lettin' the shit go", he said in his sadistically soothing tone. "Even after you killed my A-1 day one I thought 'The little nigga just did what he had to do. It was probly my fault for letting my guy get close to a job like this in the first place.'"

"Josh." I could feel myself pleading. "You just killed a fuckin' cop dawg. Just— Just chill the fuck out!"

"But here yo ass is tryna set me up? *Tsk, tsk, tsk.* It ain't have to be like this Ty.

"Josh! Just wait a minute bro. I got another fifty bands, aight? It's all you, just—"

"And Ty. Do me a favor, nigga. When I see yo ass in hell…"

"C'mon bro, chill out!"

"…don't call me Josh. My name is…

JOSHUA

AT THE NOT-SO-TENDER AGE of twelve years old, Joshua came to an ugly conclusion. The world had no use for him.

Deeper than that — the more he thought of it, the more he realized how little use he was likely to find for the world.

It wasn't something he'd learned through study or conversation. People didn't speak of it. They seemed to know off instinct that if there were a dignity to be had in life it was not to be had by him. The way ice cream and conversation are not to be wasted on stray dogs.

For starters, he wore the irreversible scarlet skin tone. He would never pass a brown paper bag test, and as a result could never expect things like empathy, patience, advantage, or forgiveness.

But blackness alone was not his curse. In fact many of his favorite people were black. Those being the ballers, rappers, hoopers and movie stars that supplied him with his very thin, and very unstable line of guidance.

And he walked that line like a tightrope.

You see, the difference between Joshua and his black idols was that he, unlike they, did not possess any worthwhile ability. He could not run, rap, act, ascertain, chose, or charm with any discernible dignity. And of these deficiencies, it was his simple social skills that made him the sorest.

He had long realized that for any black person to make their way in this world, a fair share of convincing would be required. Sadly, poor Joshua was much more muffed mouth than silver tongue, and had not seen the condition improve even in spite of his best efforts.

From time to time he'd notice folks with copper complexion and nixed knack making good in life. People like his cousin Rodney, who worked for the bank, or his neighbor Mr. Eason, who drove a very clean and well kept Saturn. But Joshua understood that for him, such an existence could only result in the compounding of his life's torture.

He knew that the very thing which made life bearable for drones like his cousin and neighbor, was the one thing he himself lacked. The cherry on top of all his debilitations, that would damn him in spite of any non-damning qualities he could develop over the course of a lifetime.

Joshua had no family.

By this I do not mean that he was an orphan, for even orphans belong to a family of orphaned people, connected and united by the tales of their shared experience. To his knowledge, there was no person with whom Joshua could compare his particular straits. His seemed to be a very special kind of alone in the world. The kind that disguised itself as being attached.

Yes, Joshua did live in a house. And that house did come equipped with its very own father, brother, mother, and sister. And like the rest of the world, this bit of information may convince you that he was in fact far from alone. But the truth was more nuanced than juxtaposition of bodies, or commonality of DNA.

Stacy, the brother he lived with, was five years Joshua's senior, and not his father's son. The sister, Amber, outranked him by eight years and was not his mother's daughter. The father Lester, and mother, Mildred, had made a decision at some point between Joshua's conception and birth, that the two of them should live out the rest of their days as mortal enemies. Not just to each other, but to their respective step children as well.

Naturally, this decision reverberated into contempt

between the two step siblings, and a resentment toward the parents who had ensnared them in such a trap.

In short, Joshua lived in a house full of hate, but to be clear, hate was not the issue. Had he received any morsel of the visceral contempt constantly flung about before his eyes, he would, for better or worse, have been inducted into the family with which he lived.

He was not.

It's often been said that there is a thin line between hate and love, but the distance between love and what Joshua felt from the people with whom he lived was more like an ocean.

Stacy, Amber, Lester, and Mildred, who despised one another more than anything in the world, were forced to endure each other's slings for one reason, and one reason alone. That being the existence of young Joshua.

It was his life that sealed the soul crushing bond between Mildred and Lester. And if not for the beating of his heart, or functioning of his lungs, the foursome of otherwise content human beings would have been free to experience true and earnest lives, far removed from the cycle of shame that passed for a so called "family".

And so in the eyes of his housemates, Joshua was not what one would consider a "son" or "brother". He was not a twelve-year-old boy. Nor had he ever been, or would he ever be a boy or man of any age. He was not a living, sentient creature to be shown any level of love or hate.

What he was, and would always be, was a lynchpin. The binding force in a pair of iron shackles, destined to be pried, hammered, and picked at, if not outright ignored for the sake of getting on with ones life.

And of the four lives that had been bound, each took its turn in testing that force, hoping that out of it they might capture some sense of freedom.

Stacy, for example, tended to derive a great deal of pride from hustling Joshua.

"I'll trade you my nice watch for your color TV", he

once offered.

The watch was of course not nice at all. It was a cheap and ugly piece of metal that Joshua only valued because he'd seen it on the wrist of someone people referred to as his older brother.

Lester on the other hand found good use for the lynchpin as an alibi. Taking Joshua on playdates with children in whom he had no interest while he had sex with their mothers. The most awkward of these encounters being with a girl named Bethany, who was Joshua's classmate.

Joshua hated to see Bethany at school, but seeing as how school ran for five days a week, at seven hours per day, the hatred came to feel more like a moot point.

In time, all of Joshua's emotions would come to feel like moot points. A trait he was well known to have in common with Mildred.

Mildred suffered from what would later be diagnosed as manic depressive disorder. A disease that caused her to unload on the lynchpin with her most fiendish thoughts and hellish nature.

Although she was the housemate who could be most closely accused of caring for the boy, it was she who hurt him most. She taught Joshua at an early age to fear the world and steer clear of the cruel and vengeful people who inhabited it.

People like Amber, who was by far and away the biggest cutthroat of the bunch.

Although his loneliness was greatly hidden from the world at large, Joshua's ineptitude was on display for all to see. He possessed no sense of personal perspective, or insight, since he was circumstantially incapable of growth in any direction. His passions were not watered, but his housemates ensured that he was well enough sedated that his fight or flight instincts could not be sharpened by any real world application. The perfect storm of mediocrity.

In his soft, un-molded state, Joshua became a beloved feeding troth for all of life's vultures.

Lester and Mildred were oft inclined to support any teacher that labeled the lynchpin as stupid, or evil, since the teachers of course spent the most time with him. And all the kids got a good laugh out of exploiting his ignorance, much in the ways that Stacy did.

But at the not so tender age of twelve years old, it seemed that fate had finally decided to place mercy on the poor child when he was sent a friend by the name of Christopher.

Christopher lived in the neighborhood, and came across the lowly lynchpin one day at the service counter of a Taco Drum.

"Quit playin' and gimmie the damn tacos!" Christopher croaked.

"I already told you tacos are two for a dollar", the cashier replied. "Don't they teach you math in school? Three quarters and a nickel ain't enough."

"How the hell you gon' talk to me about school when yo' ass is workin' here?"

"Next in line please", the cashier dismissed.

"Nah man quit playin'!"

Joshua had a high level of sensitivity toward any person experiencing cruelty. And what he saw at the service counter did not sit well with him.

"I have a quarter", he volunteered from the back of the line. "Here you go."

With the satisfaction of a first responder, Joshua approached Christopher to place the rusted coin in his hand.

At first, Christopher seemed all but stumped by the gesture. The cashier was equally shocked that any tactic would get the young loudmouth to stop talking, but Joshua immediately recognized what was going on. Christopher, much like him, was not accustomed to kindness. Especially one that was unexpected and unexplained.

"Thanks homie", he finally replied. "But fuck this fat-back half-cap minimum wage motherfucker right here. He don't deserve your bread."

With the deadliest scowl a newly minted teenager could give, Christopher hurled two stiff middle fingers to the cashier before George Jefferson strolling his way to the nearest exit.

He broke his glorious stride only to glance at Joshua and utter the words "Come on."

The sound of these words did not set forth any mechanism of logic, or reason in Joshua's mind. Only a feeling. Some innate piece of his being that led him to forego his plans for a Mexican pizza combo, and follow Christopher outside.

The boys convened on a ramp way just below the giant orange drum that marked the building. One that had been built for the sake of wheelchair accessibility, but was notoriously an area where kids would meet after school and perch themselves like pigeons on the rails to talk trash.

Christopher was quick to make himself at home, but Joshua's tender approach made clear that the custom was one he'd only witnessed from afar.

"Hey, man. I'm Chris."

"I'm Joshua."

"You got money Josh?"

"Some. Probably like eleven dollars."

"You smoke weed?"

Joshua had never seen or smoked weed a day in his life. But he definitely knew what it was. He knew because one of his favorite people was a rap star named Snoop Dogg, who, to his knowledge, was the clear cut coolest human being on the planet.

Joshua had always wanted to be cool like Snoop, and even if this opportunity came in the form of a lie, he was overjoyed at his chance to play the part.

"Yeah", he forced.

"Cool", Christopher judged as he hopped down off of the rail.

Joshua's eyes stalked after the boy as he strolled over to a nearby bike. With full awareness of the repetition

Christopher looked back and extended an offer for him to stand on the rear pegs.

"Hop on", he invited.

From a distance the bike looked to have some kind of three dimensional paint job that created an illusion of real fire, but upon closer inspection, Joshua could see that an originally red coat of paint had been beaten down to a dull orange with spots of brown rust all around.

With the same insecurity that caused him to falsify his relationship to Mary Jane, Joshua mounted the back of the bike as if it were something he had done his entire life.

The truth was that this was his absolute first time riding a bike in any capacity, and he nearly fell to the ground when Christopher peddled away.

As he gained his balance, Joshua could feel the wind pressing against his skin in a way that made him feel like he was flying. A cool, yet warming sensation that he never wanted to end. Sparks of danger and excitement danced in his stomach as light poles and pedestrians zoomed toward him before disappearing into his past.

This must be how astronauts feel, he thought to himself. Life was passing through him in a way that unfolded a perspective in his heart.

Things come and go, his conscience told him. *Nothing lasts forever.*

For the duration of their ride, Christopher hadn't spoken a single word, and Joshua couldn't have been any happier about it. He knew that conversation could only lead to the exposure of his handicap, and had every intention of making his first friendship last for as long as he possibly could.

Christopher stopped his peddling out front of an apartment complex where a group of guys sat smoking cigarillos and drinking from brown paper bags. The guys were sweaty and dusty, and all in their twenties and thirties.

Christopher couldn't have been more than a year or two older than Joshua, but showed no trepidation speaking like a grown man.

"Y'all fools on deck?" He hollered before offering to dismount his bike.

"Whatchu need?" the sweatiest, and oldest, of the group hollered back.

"The homie tryna cop", Christopher explained.

"Whatchu want homie?"

Joshua wasn't sure what he'd expected, but it occurred to him all at once that he had no idea how to negotiate a drug purchase. What was certain was that he'd need to come up with something fast if he expected to keep his newfound friendship, and possibly his life, intact.

"Weed", he declared. "I have eleven dollars."

"Well I ain't doin' no hook-ups little nigga. You can get a dime or get the fuck on."

"Don't be mad cuz yo' old ass can't do fractions", Christopher defended. "The homie just tryna get his money's worth."

"You heard what I said. You don't like it you can shop somewhere else."

Christopher shook his head at the blatant lack of customer service before turning to Joshua.

"Man just give him the ten", he conceded.

Joshua was pleasantly surprised at how easily the transaction had gone down. He'd handed over the money, and in return gotten a small wad of what looked like dirty bush leaves.

He must have stared at it for a bit too long, because one of the men started to go on about how the seeds made it more natural, and assured Joshua in the harshest possible terms that he'd gotten a quality deal.

"That's the last time I bring y'all dusty asses some new business." Christopher balked in the end.

The exchange couldn't have lasted more than a few minutes, and before Joshua knew it he was back to feeling like Superman, with the wind on his face and the world at his back.

He thought about confessing how alive he'd felt in that moment, wondering if every day in Christopher's life was this exciting, or if the experience was equally special to him.

He ultimately decided against saying anything. *'No sense ruining a perfectly good day by talking'*, Stacy would always tell him.

Besides, Joshua didn't need any confirmation that the moment inside Taco Drum had been meaningful to both of them.

Christopher pulled the bike just inside of a Leimert Park back alley. Joshua stepped down off the pegs and waited to be led inside one of the buildings, but instead was invited to sit beside Christopher on a stack of old wooden pallets.

Christopher proceeded to school Joshua on the science of how to roll a blunt. He explained that since he had provided the cigar wrapping and Joshua bought the weed, that what they were doing was called "piecing up".

Joshua wasn't sure whether or not he believed what Christopher had to say, but was comforted by the fact that his new friend could do enough talking for the both of them.

It also never felt that he was being judged for his ignorance on any of the subjects, but that Christopher simply enjoyed breaking down the details of all life's happenings.

"Clear lighters are trash because they always crack", Christopher explained as he fired up the blunt. "I mean, it's nice to know how much fluid is left, but they're not reliable, know what I mean?"

Joshua refused to blink while watching Christopher achieve the two things he'd only seen Snoop Dogg do in music videos: smoke weed, and look cool doing it. He watched the tip of the blunt radiate with life, as if it were ready to jump out and dance each time his friend inhaled. Clouds of smoke were coming and going like an undersized ecosystem at Christopher's disposal. His voice became more graveled, and his mannerisms more mannish with each puff.

It was clear at this point that what Joshua was witnessing was nothing short of a ritual in godship. Best of all his turn was only seconds away.

Joshua did everything he could to make the transition of power a peaceful one, flexing every finger when the blunt was finally bestowed upon him. He knew better than to mimic the movements Christopher had just performed. It would only be an admission that he had no technique of his own. Instead he opted to duplicate the Doggfather himself.

He pulled a heavy drag to hold between his cheeks, then parted his lips for a quick reveal before sucking all of the cloud into his lungs. He had rightly impressed himself, and maybe even Christopher, up until the moment when he felt the pinch in his ribs. Suddenly he was without control of his own body, as the smoke managed to enter his legs, ears, hair, and back. He proceeded to cough, gag, wheeze, choke, woof, hack, and commit every possible alternative to breathing, which, until a few seconds ago, he hadn't known existed.

The whole ordeal lasted about three minutes and left Joshua with a pair of watery eyes, and an unmistakable tickle in the center of his chest. Not to mention he had gotten himself higher than Vince Carter on All-Star weekend.

"You good Josh?" Christopher asked in a tone making it clear that his sudden death would be a grave inconvenience.

"Ya—" was the biggest chunk of information Joshua could bring himself to vocalize in the moment.

"You good." Chris acknowledged. A statement this time. "I'd know if you wasn't. Last month I smoked with a nigga that shit his pants. I don't smell no shit on you, so I'ma go ahead and figure you good."

Joshua exploded into what could only be referred to as a cackle. Similar to the unnerving sounds of hyenas in the wild. It was an uncontrollable joy that he couldn't put a stop to no matter how hard he tried. It also didn't help to see

Christopher laughing just as hard beside him.

After some minutes of this he realized that the sniggering was more than just the product of a good joke. Joshua was trapped in a cycle of untamable hilarity. A contagion passed from him to Christopher, then from Christopher back to him again.

In an attempt to break the cycle, Joshua stumbled away to the alley's opposite wall, but Christopher chased him down with follow up zinger.

"Hold on, man. I think I smell something. Is that a shit stain?"

The laughter was instantly multiplied, and with that it became official. Joshua had laughed harder than he ever had in his natural life. On top of that, the tickle in his chest was starting to feel like something he really enjoyed. Not something he wanted to live with for the rest of his life, but a thing to make the most of while it lasted.

The blunt made its way back into his hand a few more times, and Joshua quickly resigned himself to pacing his puffs. He listened to Christopher talk about girls, fist fights, close encounters with the law, and all of the lives he himself had yet to live.

He began to fall in love with the sensation of having someone with very warm, very soft hands cradle the brain in his skull. It made him feel safe, but at the same time very nervous. He was, after all, squatting in a run-down alley decorated by graffiti, broken glass, and stale urine.

Joshua's senses shifted back and forth between the comfort of Christopher's wild narratives, and the viable vulnerability in which they both sat, until finally the shifting was just about all he could focus on. It got to the point that Joshua could feel himself looking shifty, and set out to do as much as possible to do away with the jitters.

He went through the motions of flexing, then breathing, then rocking but non of it worked. He could sense Christopher becoming uneasy with his uneasiness. Fresh out of options, Joshua proceeded to do the one thing he rarely did in the presence of other humans. Joshua began to talk.

"Usually I don't like people." He said with an eerie sort of calm. "But you're pretty cool man."

Up until now, Christopher had been like the conductor of a roller coaster. Strapping Joshua in, then hatching a smile at the look on his face as the twists and turns joyfully robbed him of his bearings.

But in the second and a half it took Joshua to complete his statement, something had shifted. Christopher was noticing for the first time the depth with which he spoke. Not that his voice itself were deep or raspy, but that the soul behind it were somehow anchored to something buried beneath the earth. In the hours they'd spent together, Christopher had never suspected Joshua would be capable of such clarity. A kind of clarity that made him feel foolish. As if the roller coaster he'd been conducting had suddenly transformed into a seesaw.

"Thanks", he said in an attempt to match the gravity of the boy across from him.

Joshua's jitters were beginning to subside. The stages of laughter and anxiety felt far removed, and the weed was now ushering him into a state of emboldenment.

"Yeah man it's like… It's like they wanna be bad but they're scared to. Ya' know?"

"Nah. Watchya mean?"

"I mean, like— say you wanna kill somebody", he started. "You not gon' do it cuz you can't get away with it. So you do a bunch of little stuff instead. To kinda kill the person but not really. Stuff you can get away with."

For a moment he worried that he'd said too much, but was relieved to hear Christopher respond with a simple:

"Who you tryna kill?"

"Nobody", Joshua answered. "But they wanna to kill me though."

"Who?" Christopher snapped.

Joshua looked at Christopher with an evenness.

Measuring very precisely what he saw. He realized in the moment that there was no need to answer. Christopher knew exactly who. Not by shape or title, but by type. And from the clinching of his jaw, he knew that Christopher felt the same way about that who as he did, and could be relied upon for solidarity when facing all the who's of the world.

It was the final seal on what would be a very long and worthy friendship.

"Hey", Christopher said after allowing his anger drift. He pointed to the latch of the garage door behind them, noticing for the first time that it was not locked.

"This fool left his shit open."

Your Narrator, Checking In

SALUTATIONS my seedy subscriber. Have you missed me? I should certainly hope not. It isn't that I don't enjoy our one sided seminars, but it is my intention to seduce you with story, not soliloquy. And although I have yet to confess my reason for addressing you so directly, rest assured that all will be made clear by the end of our journey.

In the meanwhile, do allow me to share a bit of catharsis. After one very successful snack, your narrator has been made a newly minted member of the campus club!

You may regard us as a sinful society, fiendish fellowship, or maybe even a corroded congregation. Just please, for the love of God, do not debase your tongue with a word as witless as 'cult'. I take comfort in thinking of you as far less dense than the so-called doctors on campus, with whom I can promise you I won't be sharing anymore personal information.

You of course, my comrade in chronicle, are privy to all that I know, which as of now is as follows:

Before being mandated to our medical facilities, two of my campus mates claim to have made the acquaintance of Lucifer himself. Upon this encounter they were given what our club lovingly refers to as "the secret knowledge". These being details of human history and other worlds, of which almighty God does not want mere mortals to know. *"lest he put forth his hand and take also of the tree of life, and eat, and live for ever"* as He admonishes in the good book.

Pay no attention to the rote recital of my newly adopted dogma. It's just that I personally have always found the devil to be a bit unimpressive. Nothing but petty tricks and desperate pleas for endorsement. To be frank, I get the feeling that he doesn't even enjoy his work. And every wise man knows that power without passion is no power at all.

This does nothing, however, to detract from the appreciation of my admittance. It should go without saying that life behind the walls of a madhouse is often lacking in the way of constructive activity. Typically the most excitement one can hope to find comes in the shape of an occasional scuffle, or recounting stories of how and why some fool decided to eat his own shit.

But now! With the structure enforced by my adopted organization, your narrator has finally got actual events to look forward to. None the least of which will be the great summoning, scheduled for exactly one week from today.

As I understand it, the event will include at least three human sacrifices, and a very grand ritual that hopes to summon Mr. Lucifer to the party.

Selfishly, I must admit, I have been making work of swaying the tall man and his cohorts to extend their invitation instead to a more worthy guest. One who is always game for a good sacrifice, and whose capacity to inflict suffering is unmatched. How pure an event it would be to summon my candidate, instead of lecherous Lucifer. I should avoid naming the creature I have in mind for now. You'll have to forgive me for feeling a bit superstitious over the prospect, but if I am to have my way it will be life changing for us all. In fact...

Wait.

Apologies but... Is that the door? It's not dinner time is it?

Well hello guards. How are we this evening..? I beg your pardon? Hey! Hey, what are you doing? Get your God damn hands off of me! Let me the fuck go damn you! Do you want to end up like your man? Is that it? Because I will kill all of you! Every last One! I swear to…

KEVIN N' JOE

KEVIN N' JOE WAS DIGGIN' a hole. A big one in fact. So big they couldn't tell if it was the daytime or night.

"What time is it?" Joe asked.

"Ha'n the hell should I know!" Kevin spit back.

Ya' see, Kevin liked to consider himself a smart man, which had a way of makin' him impatient at times. And Joe was dumb, which of course meant the opposite. But all in all the two of 'em was the absolute best of friends. Though I could mention that at this particular time they was each other's only choice.

Ya' see, Kevin and Joe had been diggin' this here hole goin' on 'bout two years now, and, as a result, the hole was turnin' out to be where both of 'em lived.

"Do ya' think we call it a day?" Joe asked, whipin' the sweat from his forehead.

"I s'pose that's as good a plan as any." Kevin winced.

Somewhere 'round two years ago, these poor jokers had a lapse in judgement that got their sorry asses declared enemies of the state. The finer details are a little fuzzy, but I can tell ya' that both Kevin and Joe was big fans of a certain politician who gave 'em some bad ideas. Them bad ideas got to turnin' into some bad decisions, and well... long story short, Joe copped himself a squat somewhere inside the U.S. capitol building, and Kevin was deemed responsible for the death of a police officer.

Lookin' to avoid the heat that went along with them crimes, God bless 'em, the boys wound up diggin' themselves a hole so deep that they could literally not get out of it. 'Least, not without a little help.

"Got any beetles?" Joe asked from the pit of his belly.

"None that I'm gonna share with you'" Kevin laid out.

"Awe, come on now Kevin. Only reason you got the good stuff's cuz I was out front all day wit' the axe."

"Same reason you got the good stuff last time."

"Yeah, but last time I shared whitchya. 'Member?"

"I do not."

Another thing I should mention before goin' on wit' this story is that both Kevin and Joe was livin' every day of their lives in total darkness. Somethin' that'd driven 'em nuts at the start of their journey, but over time they learned to deal with.

Certain... "adjustments" ya' might call 'em.

And even though couldn't neither one of 'em see worth a damn, both them fellas knew sure as sugar that they were not the same as before.

Hard hands. Soft teeth. Keener noses, and ears too.

And havin' grown themselves a better sense of things in the physical, one point the boys agreed on is that wherever they was diggin' to, things was gettin' migh-tee hot.

Now, the way they looked at it was since the excursion'd nearly froze their dicks off 'round the three month mark, gettin' in good wit' the heat was a right fine idea. What they hadn't factored in was the way them adjustments'd given 'em a higher tolerance for the elements. Calcification of the skin's what it was.

"You lyin' through your teeth!" Joe hollered.

"The hell I am!" Kevin woofed.

"Kevin? You gon' sit right here'n tell me I didn't share two beetles and a hand fulla worms with you the time b'fore last we ate?"

"Why would I need to share your worms? It's worms all over the damn place!"

"Cuz you're a lazy son of a bitch, that's why."

"Oh am I?"

"Yeah. You got to be maybe the laziest man I ever met. Don't think I ain't kept track a' who done the most diggin' all this time. And the most sleepin' too."

"Yeah well that's just fine. You know what, how 'bout 'nsteadda these beetles you can help yourself to a heap'n hand fulla shit for dinner? How's that sound?"

"Sounds to me like fuck you, and fuck you Kevin! I had enough a' your ass."

Joe grabbed hold of his trusty shovel-axe and got to choppin' away at the dirt wit' a fury.

"Don't you dare follow me neither Kevin. I'm done witchu. Done as a God damn apple fritter. Or a pecan pie… or slice a' steak… damnit I miss eatin' real food!"

"An' I miss people who ain't dumb as shit. Ya' don't hear me complainin'."

"I'm serious now Kevin. I'm diggin' this way. An' you can dig your own damn hole, but don't you follow me."

"I wouldn't follow you inta Margot Robbie's pussy."

"Well nobody's gettin' any pussy now are they, Kevin? Thanks to you and your dumbass idea. 'Oh there's just so many underground bunkers these days', ain't there? 'We's just bound to luck up on one', ain't that right?"

"Maybe if the compass you packed for us wasn't on your damn cellphone."

"And just what was you gonna do wit' a compass anyhow, huh? Not like you got any clue where'n the fuck we're g…."

Right 'bout then's when the sound'a Joe's voice got to fadin' out. Further and further away 'til Kevin realized he was sittin' in that hole all by his lonesome.

No sooner'n the thought firmed up on his brain'd he get to scurryin' 'round like a hit possum in search 'a whatever sinkhole swallowed his amigo. Hootin' 'n hollerin' aside, wasn't neither one of them boys lookin to get left behind in a two year old ditch.

"Joe! Hey Joe!" Kevin yelled. "Joe, can ya' hear me? Hey man, holler so I know where y…"

And wit' a crack of the earth Kevin'd managed to slip himself right through the same crack that got Joe. By the time he's able to put two and two together he could feel his whole body fallin' through a wet and rubbery breeze.

Not the kinda fallin' that'd cause a fright, mind you. Slow and easy's how it went. Come to think of it, fallin' probably ain't even the word. Sinkin's a lot more like it. An' for some strange reason the amount of time that sinkin' took was lost on Kevin by the time his backside touched down in a patch of moss.

"Kevin! Kevin, can ya' believe it?"

Kevin lifted his head and saw Joe standin' in front of him like some kinda pruned smurf. The calcified skin had shriveled up tight, chokin' most of the hair off his head an' body. His teeth was a dirt yellow. His ears was pinned back to a point up-side his head. And his eye lids looked like a struggle to peel open. Seemed like them "adjustments" was 'bout as good as gettin' beat in the face wit' an ugly stick.

Seein's how Kevin was cooped up in the hole for as long as Joe he knew he'd have to look just as bad, if not worse. But at the end of the day he was just happy to've found his buddy. Though he was twice as curious as to what in the heck was goin' on.

Puttin' himself upright he realized for the first time that the moss he landed on was smack dab in the middle 'a some kinda forrest. Trees, marshes, vines, swamps, and the whole deal. A bit of swamp fog was cloggin' up the air, and Kevin's sight was about as sore as you could expect after livin' in the dark for two years, but there wasn't a doubt on his mind as to what he was lookin' at.

"What in the heck..." he whispered, rubbin' hard on his dried out peepers.

"I know right?" Joe was so dag gone excited, Kevin could'a swore he'd seen a tail waggin' somewhere behind him. "We must'a dug our way clear to China, Kevin. Can ya' believe it? Boy for a while there I didn't think you was gonna make it. I sure am glad ya' finally decided to follow after me."

"What're you bumpin' your jaws about?" Kevin groaned. "I fell through right after you did."

"Ya' what now? Nah, that can't be right. I know for fact it's been at least some hours, cuz the sun done went down and came back up over them mountains."

Joe aimed his pointin' finger at some hillsides off in the yonder. And sure 'nuff the tip of the sun was huggin' em all by the shoulders.

"Well I'll be." Kevin said in a low voice. Then a bitter thought came and pinned his ear upside his shoulder. He looked up and all directions before askin' "Where exactly did we fall from, Joe?"

"Ya' mean where'd I fall from or where'd you?"

Kevin wasn't exactly sure what he'd meant, but he knew he wanted Joe to give him a straight answer, and hurry the hell up doin' it.

"Well I been walkin' ever since I got here. Like I said that's at least however many hours the nighttime takes. An' then you fell somewhere behind me just a minute ago, so can't say I seen exactly where it was from. But hey, what'n hell difference does it make, right? We're finally outta that dang hole's all I care 'bout."

While Joe was helpin' Kevin up to his feet, Kevin was decidin' to agree wit' everything he was hearin'. Long as they was out and about in the free world, wasn't much use lookin' a sinkhole in the mouth.

"Guess you was aimin' to make the other side a' them hills." Kevin figured aloud. "Get yourself a feel for exactly what part a' China we wound up on?"

"You bet your ass I was", said Joe, still waggin' that imaginary tail of his.

"Well... no sense lettin' me hold ya' up. Lead the way."

Joe slapped Kevin one good time between the shoulders and hopped right to task, roundin' trees and pullin' down vines on his way to the open valley before the hills. Once they reached the end of the forrest it was smooth sailin' across, but the walk still took time. Hours in fact. And all though Kevin and Joe decided to trade looks instead a' words on the subject, both of 'em was wonderin' how in all that time the sun never came full blazin' over the sky. That if they didn't know better they'd swear it was hidin' from 'em.

Silence kept, the boys went right along soldierin' as if nothin' was amiss. And besides the fact they was about as beat as two farm mules once they passed the valley, they didn't waist an inch of time settin' foot to trudge up them hills.

There was a hard itch between the two of 'em to solve whatever's goin' on wit' that sun. One that was swimmin' 'round and takin' hold of their limbs like some kinda possession.

Feelin's of freedom and relief got to washin' clean every bone in their bodies.

Wit' the calcified skin they figured to make easy work of the climb. Joe in particular could already taste the view waitin' at the top.

Trouble was, before the boys could pull more'n a couple feet up off the ground they'd ran into somethin' they wasn't quite ready for. Somethin' that stopped 'em cold in their tracks.

"Holy shit", Kevin snapped. "It's a God damned Leopard!"

It sure'n'a hell was. A big ass one too. The boys stood 'bout stiff as two corpses wonderin' if they was gonna wind up bein' dinner before they got breakfast. Joe looked over to Kevin for some kinda answer, but all he could make out was the sweat wellin' up on back of his neck.

"Maybe...uh..." Joe was doin' what he could to think on his feet. "Maybe if we move reeeeeeel slow... we might find a way around it."

The boys went ahead and gave it the best shot they could, but there wasn't much use. No matter how slow they moved the leopard was only gettin' meaner an' meaner wit' every step. An' no sooner'n they got themselves a little distance, a big ol' white lion and a grey wolf came walkin' up beside it.

"Aww, ain't this a bitch!" Joe let out.

In no time at all the leopard, lion, and wolf had formed themselves a perimeter near the bottom of the hill. As if they was all in cahoots a' makin' sure the boys couldn't reach the top.

"Kevin are you seein' this?" Joe asked.

"Don't know how I could miss it. These the first critters you met since gettin' here?"

"First and only"

Before Kevin or Joe could hatch themselves a plan on how to handle their predicament, that grey wolf got to stalkin' toward 'em. It was howlin' and growlin' and doin' what it could to make clear that it had zero intention on bein' friendly. The boys caught wind of the message and decided to hi-tail it back down for the valley just as quick as they could.

But when they landed down off the hill to where the valley should'a been the absolute damndest thing happened. They realized that they wasn't in the valley. They was right back in the middle of the woods. Kevin could even recognize the patch a' moss he first landed on, seein's how it was still wearin' his butt print.

"Kevin", Joe tip toed. Where exactly might ya' guess we are? I mean, if you was a bettin' man?"

Kevin was 'bout as close to speechless as Joe'd ever seen. He spent a long time with his jaw hangin' loose and his eyes fixed on the moss before answerin' "Not China" in a real serious voice.

"Ah-Ha-Ha-Ha-Ha!"

As if Kevin had told some sorta joke, a deep crisp laugh came cuttin' through the air. But it wasn't comin' from him or Joe. It was somewhere in the distance. Behind the trees n' fog. A piece a' shadow that was gettin' bigger n' uglier the closer it got. Kevin n' Joe squinted real hard tryna get that shadow to turn into somethin' they could recognize. When the light finally did pull across the damn thing it wasn't nothin' either of 'em could say they seen before, but somehow someway both the boys knew exactly who and what they was lookin' at.

What was standin' in front of 'em had the shape of a man, but was over nine feet tall wit' eyes like a goat, skin like a snail, and baboon fur coverin' its arms. It was skinny as all get out but still bulgin' wit' veiny muscles everywhere they looked includin' its face, which, coincidentally, might'a been the ugliest the boys'd ever seen. An' if the damn thing wasn't scary enough on its own, it was carryin' the torso of a dead dog in its big ol' claw-lookin' hand. Takin' bites outta the chest like an apple. Years of malnutrition's about the only thing kept Kevin n' Joe' from shittin' their pants right there on the spot.

"Hey guys, sorry I'm late." The beast said wit' about six voices at once. It held the dog torso up, drippin' blood out where the boys could see. Then gave 'em an easy shrug. "Late lunch", he said.

"Jesus, Mary, Joseph, and Bob, it's the God damn devil!" Joe broke down to his knees and started prayin' like a whore at a baptism. "Oh I'm so sorry lord! Please father in heaven forgive me for takin' that shit! I swear I'll never do it again!"

"Hey", the beast roared. "Knock that shit off… Seriously. He will hear you."

"I want him to hear me! An' you hear me too damn devil. I rebuke you motherfucker!"

"Oh really?"

"Yeah. Really."

"You rebuke me?"

"You bet your damn ass I do. Rebuke, repent, whatever'n a hell it takes to get your butt back in that forrest and the hell away from us."

"You know I pulled a lot of strings to get you inbred motherfuckers down here? You're not even dead yet."

"We ain't?" Kevin peeped with a spark a' joy.

"No", the Beast answered. "And for the record this isn't even hell, alright? It's the forrest of fuck ups. I came here to help your dumb asses get back to your regular lives. But since we're out here "rebuking" each other? You two can figure your own way out. Good luck."

Now Joe seemed well enough wit' lettin' the Beast get on about his business, but Kevin already had his wheels spinnin' on a more pragmatic approach.

"Hold on now there Mr. Devil, Satan, Lucifer, sir." He started in a voice made for bargainin'. "Now're you sayin' you can call off them rabid critters on the hillside? Get us a way through?"

"Critters?" The Beast responded. "You mean the leopard, lion, and, she-wolf?"

"That I do. Do ya' happen to keep some sorta cage, or whoopin' stick might get 'em out the way?"

"Yeah, that's a no-go. I mean technically I could go over there and rip 'em to shreds but they'd only keep coming back to life. Plus keeping guys like you from reaching the top of that hill is kinda their job so..."

"Well then how exactly do we get outta these dang woods? Far's I done seen that's the only way."

"Which is exactly why you need a guide", the Beast offered. "All we've gotta do is take a little trip through hell and—"

"I knew it!" Joe piped. "I right, dang knew it, Kevin, this son of a bitch is anglin' to rob us a' our eternal souls!"

"Woah there buddy." The Beast said with a light chuckle. "There's no robbery going on here. Your souls are already spoken for. Sorry to spoil the ending, but I thought that part was kind of obvious.

"But ya' just said we wasn't dead yet?" Kevin whined.

"And you're not. Or at least you don't have to be. The year 2022 is your scheduled death date. There's nothing I can do about that. But what I can do is send you both back. To when you first started digging the hole? You'd get to do the last two years over, and when you do come to hell, I'll roll out the red carpet. I can even get you guys jobs. You like fucking shit up don't you?"

Kevin n' Joe shared a rightly suspicious look between the two of 'em. The boys wasn't exactly sure how to take what was bein' said, much less give any kinda response. Kevin could see it all over Joe's face that he'd rather climb right back in the hole they fell from before goin' through hell, but was too shook to pipe up and say anything.

The Beast must'a picked up on the thoughts they was havin', because he followed his offer up wit' just the piece of clarification they needed.

"Or you can get started on eternal damnation right now. It's your call."

"Just what's in it for you?" Joe demanded.

"A favor for a favor. I give you a pass in hell, you give me one when you're back on earth."

"Us?" Kevin wondered aloud. "Well I'm not quite sure where it is ya' git your facts from, but me n' ol' Joe here's just regular boys. Now if what you're after is somebody wit' the resources or experience to accommodate a feller like yourself there's a cunt bitch named Hillary I'm pretty sure you already know."

"HA HAHA HA HA…" The Beast right about killed over wit' that deep and prickly laugh a' his, makin' Kevin feel about the size of a flea in a lion's den for pipin' up. He and Joe couldn't help but to look at each other wit' an even deeper sense of defeat.

"Come on now guys", the Beast bellowed. "Give yourselves some credit. You're humans! Made in the image of the man himself. All you gotta do is perform one little ritual and we'll be good. I'll give you everything you need to make it happen."

The boys weren't exactly thrilled wit' the offer, but there was nothin' they could do to fight it. The Beast had 'em right by the souls. Kevin, ever the con man, leaned right in with his hand out.

"We got a deal?" The Beast asked.

"Deal", Kevin confirmed.

"Deal wit' the gat danged devil." Joe muttered to hisself, kickin' dirt n' tearin' up all the while.

"He gonna be alright?" The Beast asked Kevin.

"Probly just needs a little time for it to sink in" he reasoned. "Two more years a' livin' plus we skip the fire an' torture when we get back here. That's what you're offerin'?"

"You guys will practically be running the place", the Beast told him.

Kevin and the Beast looked over to Joe, who was too busy talkin' himself into an ulcer to chime in. "I promise I will never go number two again. No sir-eee. Long as I got butt cheeks to clinch, I do not care..."

"Maybe we oughtta give him a couple minutes to settle down?" Kevin suggested.

"Are you kidding?" The Beast laughed. "He's gonna fit right in."

Without missin' a beat, the snail-skinned fella got to walkin' off through the woods. Joe and Kevin, bein' all outta options, went ahead and tailed right on behind him. Along the way the boys did their fair share of complainin' — yippin' n' yappin' about sore feet n' heavy backs. But the Beast never did hesitate to remind 'em what all the walkin' was about in the first place.

"Man, it's a good thing you guys lucked up on this deal", he'd tell 'em. "If a little walking wears you down you wouldn't last five minutes of hell torture. Well, technically you'd last all of eternity, but it would suck so bad."

And if the boys was ever bold enough to ask for a break the Beast'd just get to pokin' fun wit' comments like "I thought you country boys walked everywhere?" Or "you mean to tell me you spent two years digging a hole, but can't handle a few days on your feet?"

The whole time this went on Kevin n' Joe couldn't help feelin' like their guide was gettin' his kicks outta makin' 'em suffer. It was, after all, his nature to torture souls, and torture was the exact word to describe the path they'd took.

But, after a few hard days the trip' was finally done, and just like the Beast promised, Kevin n' Joe found themselves standin' before the real live gates of hell. Before even havin' set foot inside they was hearin' the wails and moans of the damned souls behind it. There was a sign sittin' over top the gates, but the message was written in a language the boys'd never seen before. The Beast caught 'em gawkin' an' took time to translate one section in particular:

SACRED JUSTICE MOVED MY ARCHITECT.
I WAS RAISED HERE BY DIVINE OMNIPOTENCE.
PRIMORDIAL LOVE AND ULTIMATE INTELLECT.

The boys wasn't quite sure what to make a' them hundred dollar words, but the Beast assured he'd explain it all when the time was right. For now, their journey through hell was gettin' under way.

Kevin n' Joe followed their guide through the not so pearly gates, and no sooner'n they made their way cross, a feelin' of hollow pain was gnawin' at their bellies. A contagion a' hurt n' sufferin' that rode the back of black dust fillin' the air. A dust kicked up by whatever was rumblin' deep inside the ground.

Kevin looked down over what had to be the biggest pit he'd ever seen n' saw what looked like every human on earth runnin' 'round in one big circle. They was all jumbled up on top of one another, doin what they could to try n' collapse from being so dang exhausted, but it just wasn't no kinda room for fallin' down.

Right smack in the middle of that eternal lap was a wasps nest 'bout the size of the Eiffel Tower. The wasps flew 'round stingin' the hell outta everybody in the pit 'til they bled somethin' terrible. N' all the runners had their feet and legs covered in maggots that were eatin' after the blood.

Kevin stood starin' at it all for a minute or so, too disgusted to look away. Before he knew it his face was full of tears and the ground in front of him was wearin his last drop a' stomach juice. The cryin' and beggin' of a billion souls was about the last thing he heard before passin' out.

"Kevin!" Joe yelled.

"Don't worry about it", the Beast assured. "Happens to the best of 'em. Here, you grab the legs."

Like a couple a' frat boys, Joe and the Beast lugged Kevin on over to the bank of a nearby river.

"So that's hell, huh?" Joe asked the Beast.

"Not yet, no. This is more of a lobby situation. All the people who didn't want to pick a side when it came to good and evil. The punishment for indifference."

Without thinkin' Joe dropped his half of Kevin to the ground n' stared up at the Beast like a terd on a horse.

"Indifference!" He hollered. "You get all that just for indifference?"

"One thing I've learned in my time on this job...", the Beast said, tossin' Kevin's limp body up over his shoulder. "...ignorance is the deadliest sin there is."

For reasons big and small that idea sat real heavy on Joe's heart. All at once he was beginnin' to realize that outta all the sufferin' he'd done over his life, the absolute worst came at times when he just didn't know any better. Even now he couldn't help but to wonder who he'd a' been if his trip to hell came a lot sooner on.

Joe stared at the back of the Beast's head while the Beast stared out at the river. He wondered to himself why a planet full of souls would get left guessing what to do for a few decades just to spend all eternity suffern' for gettin' it wrong.

The Beast looked back at Joe over his shoulder and gave him a slow wink. Joe couldn't help feelin' comforted by the gesture. The Beast was beginin' to make a whole lotta sense to him, much in the ways Kevin always did. Kinda like a friend.

"This guy's kind of a dick" the Beast warned. "Just let me do the talking."

In the most serendipitous of fashion an old row boat

came visible through the river's fog. The captain of that ship was a fella 'bout as black as the night around him. He had white hair and spinin' balls of fire where his eyeballs should'a been. Joe couldn't help but notice the looseness in the man's jaw, which's seemed to be makin' every word he spoke more trouble'n it was worth.

"Ahhh, you done fucked up now!" The dark man yelled. "Bet' not one a' you goofy bastards ask me where you're at neither cuz you already know. No take backs, no make ups, and no second chances, you dumb shits. Y'all had your shot. Now hurry up and get on this boat 'fore I lose my motherfuckin' cool."

Joe followed the Beast in a huddle of very depressed faces that looked to be under some sorta spell. It was obvious that nobody, including Joe, wanted to get on that boat, but all the same the crowd was movin' along smooth as butter. The dark man's face snapped toward Joe, and with that lose jaw hollered "Who the fuck are you?" Then he turned to Kevin up on the Beasts shoulder 'n said "and what the fuck is that?"

"Relax, Charon", the Beast said. "These two are with me."

"I don't give a fuck who they with. I can hear their guts pumpin' and squishin' all the way from here. They ain't gettin' on my boat."

"Oh sorry. Should I go get Virgil to read you a poem?" The Beast teased. "Maybe me and the guys can put on a little talent show for you?"

"Fuck you! Why you wanna go and bring up Virgil, huh? You know damn well that slick talkin' motherfucker made his way through more'n just me! Not to mention he was sent here by somebody with way higher clearance than you."

Joe couldn't help but notice how Charon's last comment seemed to rub the Beast the wrong way. So much so that the ugly son of a bitch turned around to Joe and dropped Kevin right plum in his arms.

"Hold this", he said before squarin' his shoulders up on

Charon.

Before Joe could wrap his head around what was what, the Beast was layin' hands claws, teeth, and horns into Charon's frail old body, spillin' bile and guts every which way he could imagine. With the same claw of a hand Joe saw him carryin' the dead dog, the Beast ripped Charon's loose jaw right off his face and started beating him in the head wit' it. Tearin' into the poor bastards skull with his own teeth.

Strange enough Charon seemed to be more annoyed than hurt by the violence of it all. Joe couldn't understand exactly why, but to see that kinda tolerance for pain made him bubble up wit' an awful kinda jealousy. Whether it was his own repressed nature, or the stench a' hell that did it to him, Joe felt that jealousy spark and flare into a white hot hatred. An uncontrollable passion that had him stompin' his own foot inta Charon's chest and balls. Throwin' punches and hurlin' cuss words quicker'n he could say his own name.

"Joe!" Kevin yelled. "What'n the hell'r ya' doin'?

Joe looked over his shoulder and saw Kevin was finally startin' to come round from his nap. Funny thing was ol' Joe was feelin' about the same way seein's how he couldn't seem to recall exactly when he'd put his buddy down. Or when the Beast'd picked him up for that matter. He watched wit' a jaw about as loose as Charon's as Kevin twisted his way down outta those veiny grey arms.

The Beast had himself a twisted kinda smile watchin' Joe watch him — tryna piece together when exactly it was the two of 'em had traded places.

"But I... you just..." Joe fumbled and bumbled his words around before finally lookin' down at his hand, which he'd already come to figure was holdin' Charon's jaw.

"What'n'a fuck!" he exclaimed.

Charon was quick to snatch back the bottom half of his face and fasten it to his cheeks like a chin strap.

"Mothafucka'!" He shouted. You know who you dealin' wit', bitch? You wanna ride so bad how 'bout I snatch the heart out yo' chest and throw you in the fuckin' hole right now?"

Joe was too busy tryna figure exactly when he lost track of his body to answer the question.

"That's a pretty big rule to break Charon." The Beast eased in. "Something tells me he wouldn't be the only one in that hole if you did."

Charon gritted his teeth about the best he could knowin' good and well how right the Beast was. Then he pointed them fiery eyeholes of his square at Joe and made a decision.

"Aight then Mr. Joe", he said wit' a rumble so low it could put goosebumps on a rattlesnake.

Both the boys was taken aback to find out that the boatman even knew Joe's name. Though things had long gotten to a point they weren't sure how much further back they could be took.

"I ain't gonna kill ya", Charon went on. "Matter 'fact ima take your dumb ass exactly where you wanna go. And when we get there I'm lettin' eeeeverybody know who the fuck you is, and who the fuck you ain't."

Well 'course a threat like that comin' out of a hellspawn like Charon left poor Joe standin' blue in the face and soft in the waist. The Beast didn't make one lick a' effort to hide how satisfied he'd been wit' the outcome as he came by slappin' him on the shoulder.

"Don't worry buddy. I got your back", he grumbled.

"The fuck he does!" Charon barked in response as Kevin and Joe joined all the damned souls loadin' up on the wooden boat.

The ride 'cross that river went ahead and got under way, and lemme tell ya' that the time it took was not at all what you'd call easy. For starters there was a strong chorus of wailin' and beggin' from all them damned souls still hopin' to avoid their eternity of hell torture. And that chorus swam 'round in circles over the boys ears. So much so that they'd all but lost track of whether or not they was still just passin' through or on the startin' blocks of a full time residence. Not to mention the buck naked feelin' Joe had in the pit of his belly after loosin' control a' hisself wit' Charon. Or the heavy ball of guilt rollin' back and forth on Kevin's shoulders for not bein' awake to stop it from happenin' in the first place.

On top of all that the boys wasn't too thick to notice Charon and the Beast havin' themselves some kinda secret negotiation off in the corner. Joe in particular was tits up tryna decide if it was good or bad that the two of 'em was gettin' along.

Somewhere in the middle of the boys havin' what had to be the saddest starin' contest a feller could see, somethin' downright unexpected happened. A plot twist they wasn't quite prepared to take. Somewhere deep along in that chorus a' wails, one of the damned souls decided to straighten up and take themselves a solo.

"Don't believe them!" The sufferin' voice cut through.

The boys turned their heads like two chickens at a feed to find themselves bein' stared at by a woman. One that was obviously young, but somehow managed to walk around lookin' twice her own age. She was half dressed wit heroine bites all up and down her arms, and bruises from a beatin' so bad you'd have to figure it the thing that landed her there on the boat.

The young old hag looked to be shakin' herself outta that spell that had all the others, and anybody watchin' could tell it was real work for her takin' the few steps she did in the boys' direction.

"This place...", she growled wit a voice more hollow than the hell wind around 'em. "It is a prison only to us... to them!" She snapped her finger fast as a bull whip pointin' to Charon and the Beast. "For you it is a path. Carved out by the greatest of men, thousands of years ago. Do not be led astray. You are not lost. You... have time. If you stay the course... if you learn from the sins of the damned you will reach heav—"

'Bout quicker than you could snap a turkey's neck the Beast had that big ol' claw lookin' hand a' his wrapped around the hag's face, and was squeezin' just as hard as he could. Kevin and Joe watched like two sick puppies while he went on to pop her head like a watermelon. An ugly piece of business, lemme tell ya'.

The boys was so stunned that they didn't stir back to life 'til realizin' that even wit' a cracked skull and loose brains the hag still wasn't dead. Least no more'n she already had been. For them it was the most terrifyin' sight of their lives watchin' that poor woman scream and twitch as she bled out on the deck, seemin' to feel every inch of the damage the Beast had done.

Must be the case that even a dead person needs their brain because after a while the twitchin' got pretty violent. She was flappin' round like a trout on the deck and speakin' in crazy tongues by the time Charon came and stood over her.

"What the hell was that?" He hollered.

"You know", the Beast replied.

It was the closest either of the boys had come to seein' that nine foot son of a bitch bein' afraid since they'd first met up in the woods.

A crack like that in the Beast's nature right after the woman's message had Joe and Kevin sittin' deep in the yolk of choice for the rest of the boat ride. It was the choice of choice, if ya' know what I mean.

See the boys could figure about as well as you or me what that ugly hag was tryna get across. Just like they was only a head's turn from realizin' who'd sent 'em the message. The only one they could think of to put a tickle of fear in that Beast's belly. The question at hand was did they want to know?

Tough as the road had been up to this point, Kevin, and Joe especially, had the luxury of following someone else's lead. All the way back to the politician that'd first gotten 'em started. But if they was gonna let themselves chew up and swallow that message, it'd put 'em out on their own in a way that felt too real for comfort.

They'd be makin' themselves two of the strongest enemies they possibly could in the Beast and Charon. And doin' it in the toughest place to survive in all of existence bein' actual hell. Neither of 'em had any clue about how long a journey like that would take, what it would take, or if they even had what it took to take it.

When the boat finally docked from river to shore the boys hadn't the slightest clue on where their first step should land. For Kevin the choice got a little easier when he looked up.

"Welcome to Limbo, boys!" The Beast welcomed. "The first official ring of hell, but the last you need to see."

Kevin's head took a long dry turn from his lap to the new shore he was comin' up on. Even wit' them calcified eyelids the sight he saw managed to put a slap of excitement across his face.

Joe on the other hand was too deep in his own contemplation to give off signs of life. Even wit' Kevin tappin' and pattin' at his shoulder.

"Joe! Joe, you ain't gonna believe this shit here man look!"

When Joe finally did lift his chin to see what Kevin was yappin' bout he just couldn't believe it. What the Beast'd referred to as the first rung of hell was shaped an awful lot like the mansion from he and Kevin's favorite childhood show The Beverly Hillbillies.

"This don't look like hell at all", Kevin said wit' a spark of hope.

"This here's what they call 'the in between'" Charon offered. The boys took his sudden friendliness as a byproduct of that gum chewin' he and the Beast did on the ride over. "If ya' lived a good enough life but never accepted god, this is where you end up.

"God", the Beast scoffed. "Who needs him, am I right?"

The boys took a good long look at the hag still floppin' on the deck and decided not to answer.

The Beast led 'em past the mansion to a far corner and handed over two shovels.

"Dig."

As the boys dug they noticed a light behind the mansion.

"That must be the path that woman was talkin' bout", Kevin whispered.

Joe pretended not to hear him and just kept on diggin'.

"Joe? Well didn'tcha hear what I said. We can make a run and get ourselves into heaven"

"Can ya' guarantee that?" Joe asked.

"You know just as well as I do who sent that woman, Joe."

"Yeah the same one who built this place. Dontcha see Kevin? It's all a scam. Just like Obama and the gat damn Clinton's. He makes promises to your face then kicks your ass just as soon as ya' turn around. That's what the sign was sayin' when we first walked in."

"You don't know that. That big gray motherfucker could be lyin'."

"Is everything we seen here a lie, Kevin? I mean look at where we're at. The punishment for not knowin' God is to never meet him? What did any a' these people do wrong besides bein' too dumb to know better? Let's just face facts. He's a damn child."

"But he sent us the message."

"Yeah sure, once we're already in hell. When he thinks we're too weak to fight back or choose for ourselves. Where was he when I was eight years old getting' whooped by a switch everyday, huh? Nowhere. But you came in real life Kevin. You were a real friend. Ya' taught me things, good or bad, you cared enough to be there. And all I know is that when we was eatin' bugs in a ditch that goat faced devil is the one came n' got us. He took the chances and he made the effort."

Kevin let Joe's words do a good bit a' marinatin' on his brain. For some reason that light at the tunnel felt a whole lot bigger'n what his friend had to say, but a whole lot smaller'n how familiar the two of 'em was to each other. He saw the passion on his buddy's face and the sweat from his hard work. As bad as Kevin wanted to see what was on the other side of that light he couldn't imagine it bein' more valuable than the time he and Joe'd spent together.

After takin' one last long look past the mansion he lifted his shovel up high and forced it deep down in the dirt. He was gonna take one last trip with his amigo. Far from hell and whatever was past that light. Kevin n' Joe was headed right back to the…

frontline

frontline

SHIA was bleeding bad. Coughing it up. Leaking it out. At this point he couldn't even feel where the bullets hit. Just cold. Real cold.

"Fuck off me nigga!"

Even with the life leaving his veins he still had his vision. He could see the bodies clashing all around him. Flares sparking off nozzles. Bats and knives covered in red goo. It was war. It was hell. And it was the last thing he'd ever see.

He knew the decision he made in this moment would be the last of his life, so he chose wisely. He made the choice not to think of his daughter. Of his mother standing over his dead body. The places he'd never traveled. The food he'd never taste. Shia made the choice not to cry.

That if any of his homies caught sight of his last moments they would not see shame or weakness. They would see a warrior. A symbol of strength and courage. He had frontlined a war, and his death, for better or worse would always—

"Wake up nigga! Wake up! Hey, y'all come help! Shia hit! We gotta get him to a doctor!"

Jason was slapping him hard in the face. Doing what he could to keep his friend alive. Shia didn't judge. Jason still had a lifetime of decisions beyond today's tears.

Unfortunately, Shia couldn't join him in his mourning.

"Aye Jason we gotta go!" Eric yelled. "The cops is comin' we can't be here! We gotta go!"

"I'm not leavin'. Fuck that shit I ain't leavin' him here like this."

"Go..." Shia whispered. No one could hear.

"Fuck that, I ain't leavin'. I ain't leavin'! Fuck off me nigga!"

"Quit actin' fuckin' stupid! He gone!"

Gone

Gone

Gone

Gone.....

I TRY to savor them. These last few breaths before the darkness overtakes my lungs. But it's no use. My body won't let me ignore the panic. The sweat. The tremors. The mucus forcing itself from my nose and mouth.

I think my ears are bleeding. Hard to tell at this point. My hearing is definitely gone, but that much I expected. Sound is always the first to go.

Coming down from the light is never fun, but the time I spend with my own body, actually feeling the world around me… well… I don't need to explain it to you, do I?

Run.

I need to run, can you keep up? Sorry, this is all still new to me. I hope we don't lose each other.

Right now I can still see. Sight's the last to wear off. That's why we call it light.

I'm still coughing. It's hard but I want to feel as much as I can before the darkness takes over. You have no idea how much it sucks to be trapped in thoughts all the time. No taste no smell no touch. Just darkness and the things it does to your mind.

Which reminds me. I've been meaning to ask why—

Fuck.

Agh.

I just got hit by a car.

Good news is my sense of touch already wore off. Bad

news is I'm gonna need a doctor.

Bad.

Pain.

Hurt.

You fucked up.

Don't mind that. It's the darkness telling me I'm hurting. Once the thoughts creep in I know the light's about to wear off. Give me a sec while I look at the sun, will ya'?

Hmm. Pretty.

Think I told you last time that smoking light is very illegal here, so fuck a doctor right now. Don't want them finding that shit in my system. I'm almost home anyway.

Man you should've felt the people around me when I got hit. The darkness was fucking buzzing. It was a shit show.

I'm still not sure how to transfer my physical experiences to you. Or if I can. Is that a thing with astral projection?

Oh yeah. Before I got hit I was gonna ask. Why do you come here? I mean, I get that you're trapped in some kind of nut house, but why not visit a world that's more fun? Is it like a you're crazy so you can only visit crazy realities sort of thing? Drug addicts like me?

Forget it, I'm rambling. Sorry.

You wanted to know about my world right? Well it started off a lot like yours.

Thousands of years ago the people of earth destroyed its atmosphere, allowing the dark matter of space to flood the planet. And while many had predicted the happening, none were prepared for the aftermath.

What we once believed to be a benign universe actually exists within a single ocean of living black gas. The oldest and largest organism now known to man, whose only purpose is to bind and control all that it touches.

Before the happening, earth and humanity were protected from the entity by a firmament, a field of precise energy that worked much like an embryonic sack around the globe. In those days man lived free from the omnipotent void of infinity. A garden of Eden as it were.

But over time their isolation became their downfall.

In my lifetime the darkness is all I've known. From the first time I drew breath until just a few days ago the black matter in my lungs was all that allowed me to detect my surroundings. I, like every other human today, had no idea that we were living in total ignorance.

Lungs slow.

Breathing bad.

Blood inside.

Shit.

I gotta move man. I think the darkness is trying to tell me I'm dying or something. Turns out I was right about my ears.

You might not want to stick around for this. I'm not sure how it works. If I die right now do you die too?

Move.

Move!

Fuck I can't move right now! You should really go man. The light's never done this to me before. I think the darkness—

Him.

Make leave.

What the— holy shit it's you? You're doing this you fucker? You set me up?

Why...

Lungs

Okay, let me go please I can't breath. I can't. Why would you...

Your Narrator, On Drugs

I HAVE BEEN drugged, trusted reader. The punishment for my crime against that pitiful young guard has been a barbaric raping of my guiltless mind. Fucked from all sides within these wretched walls. The pills, the isolation, the forced rhetoric, the mandated labor is all one big crude dry fuck!

In and out and in and out of the creases that line my brain are their uncircumcised doctrine. The doctrine of philistines!

Tell me, lucid lector, who owns the onus for my offense more than the creator of this world? That would cast me out of purity for some cruel lesson in the homily of his own twisted initiation!?

He is a sadist, I promise you. But my own revelation is near. A truth buried within the origins of secret knowledge, brought to us from the seventh rung of insanity by our dear brother Joseph.

There is a creature who knows the purest evil. Who has suffered directly at its hands. Have you figured it out yet, sad scholar? Do you know the tall man? Has his quiet visited your mind? If not yet, I can assure you he will. Your continued consumption of these chapters is all that's required.

And then, it is true. That we've shared the same poison,

you and I. The same hate filled needle that turns my thought swims within your blood.

Tell me? What was it for you? The right or the left arm? No matter. Rest assured that the Madness has already taken its root. You should have turned back when I gave you the chance. But you were just too cool, weren't you? Now here you are… with me. Suffering.

Does it bring you joy trusted reader? The sting of knowing? Knowing… that you are… naked?

I do hope that my current state of mind does not deceive you. That the madness does not make you frightened. It is after all your true salvation. If you should gain nothing else from my ramblings today, please, allow yourself this one bit of clarity. That at its core, madness is absolute truth. And all truth awaits us who choose to embrace it.

SUNSHINE

♫ Have my love when the sun shines. ♫

Sun shines.   Sun shines. ♪

"You ever think about how good it feels to let the sun touch you?"

Tilly ran her fingers through the green grass, stroking and massaging each blade. Careful not to cause any tears.

Her favorite cassette tape was holding up just fine in Eddie's stereo. She couldn't remember why she'd ever been so worried about it in the first place.

♪ Be mine when the sun shines.
Sun shines.   ♫

"It's almost like… God's voice? No?"

A cool wind played in her hair, nudging a flimsy t-shirt to hug all the right places.

"Aw, that's the mushrooms talkin', baby", Eddie

offered. "Gettin' ya' in tuned wit' the elements like ya' s'posed to be."

Of course he was right. Tilly was seeing the world in a way she never had before. The colors, the sounds, even Eddie. Everything was making sense. Everything was... everything.

'Eddie?' She pulled. 'Why'd you bring me here?'

'Well why not? Ya' havin' a good time ain'tcha?'

'I am', she assured. 'It's just— you've never been romantic with me before. Not that that's what you're doing now, or, I don't know if it is or not. It feels like it at least. I only ask because— Well, you and me are already fucking. And not just each other. I'd really hate to ruin things by tryna to make more out of it.'

Eddie took time to consider what was being said to him. Everything about the moment wore proof of his efforts to please the girl he was with, from their secluded location to the hard to procure psychedelics that had her speaking so freely. Even 'God's voice' seemed to betray his intentions.

'But'cha havin' a good time?' he highlighted.
'I am', she affirmed.

♫ *Diggin' on life when the sun shines.*

"Ya' know? Speakin' a fuckin', baby…"

She searched his lips for the whispers of her daydreams. His tongue for the gleam of silver that tickled her throat. Tilly never knew her secret lover to be much in the way of looks or romance, but Eddie could force a climax like nobody's business.

"What you get outta dealin' wit' them tricks anyway?"

"Tricks?" She replied with a sudden shift. "The hell you mean tricks?"

"C'mon now baby. Any nigga you got outside'a me's a stone sucka' and you know it."

"Uh-uh. No, cuz you over here talkin' about a trick and fuckin' like I'm some kinda hoe. That ain't what this is."

"Now why you gotta go and use a word like that? Ain't no need blowin' ya' high. We just talkin'."

"Mmm-hmm", she hummed with a brow raised in defense. "Eddie. If you don't knock it the hell off."

"You just mad I'm right is all. But the problem ain't got nothin' to do wit' ol' Eddie. Nah. It's them other niggas got you stressed. But see now dig this. What if all them fools comin' 'round tryna get somethin' from ya' started doin' a little givin' of they own? Gettin' ya' right like they should?"

"Like a trick?"

"Like a disciple, girl. Like when a man goes to the alter of God, or— or Buddha. Krishna, Allah. He don't show up empty handed do he? Nah. He know full well if he want that blessin' he got to get down and dig deep in his pockets. Now don't a motherfucka' leave yo' bed feelin' strong? Like he could conquer the world?"

The world? She thought. *What a thing to say?*

The blades of grass were now swimming unchaperoned between Tilly's fingers. She felt herself losing track of them and Eddie as she made room for his lofty idea.

The world?

Feelings and visions invited themselves to her inner mind, where pride and judgement stood ready to greet.

She questioned how so many of the men in her life were so rarely poised to satisfy. How only Eddie had been able to apply the fine art of shock and danger as a means of getting her off.

"Now if a man can get that feelin' from you, but can't give it back? Seems ta' me that man should be bringin' a little… *balance* to the situation."

"You give it to me Eddie. Every time we make love. Every time you talk you find a way to make me feel better than I knew on my own."

"Well I do what I can when I can, sweet heart. But I think we both know ya' deserve a whole lot more. And baby, if more is what ya' really after? I can show ya' how to make them other niggas act right."

If the sun shines... ♪

The wind ran cold and sharp over Tilly's legs. Another day filled with night. Another night gnawing at the lobes of her ears, guarding for any hint of the voice she'd felt on her picnic with Eddie.

It was months since the stroke of soft pastures grazed her palm, but not a single day that hadn't begun with its memory. A dream amongst dreams, fleeting in the wake of new and bullying wisdoms.

Wisdoms like the scent of cocaine.

A blue Buick groaned itself into the parking lot of the Bougie Squirrel. The toothy smiles of two white men gleaming eagerly through its windshield.

She was shocked to find herself frozen at the sight. An uncharacteristic flash of helplessness that proved only to invigorate the men's fervor.

They stalked toward her with long strides. Eyes piercing wild in the night like a pair of lean-bellied dogs, freely spewing their profane demands as if she were game in their hunt.

She knew that these men had not come for sex. No. These were sadists, who's only desire was to cast their flinching pains onto whatever innocent body they could find.

A prayer took shape in the fold of her heart. Silently she begged for the God of somehow to swoop in and perform his magic.

Make it stop, somehow. Turn me loose, somehow. Kill these perverts before I have to do this, somehow.

The men's smiles grew wide at the smell of her desperation as she clung tight to the visions of green grass and sunshine that had led her here.

In the wake of her hesitation a more ambitious whore came in to intercept the two crackers.

'This ain't right', she thought.

She watched as the three of them entered a room, slamming the door hard behind.

Relief grabbed her by the chest, and when she exhaled, a small cloud of her aching soul was made visible in the night air.

In a flash the longing for lost joy raced up her spine. The back of her skull tingling violently with desires that had long laid dormant, but now all at once demanded satisfaction.

'Go', a voice commanded.

She knew that this, and only this was her moment to chance it. To leave and never reenter the life that had managed to ensnare her once free spirit.

But no sooner than she turned her back, were the voices beginning to beckon.

"Tilly? Tilly, you leavin'?"

Her sister whores were no doubt looking to hold her accountable. Eddie made it painfully clear that there was no such thing as a good excuse to abandon post, and even the slightest disobedience would be met with his full displeasure.

"Tilly?"

But what choice did she have? Stay or go, the cold grip of death had already begun its reach in her direction. The only real option was to have her choice of executioner —

an enraged Eddie, or her own tormented self?

"Is that you?"

Fuck it.

"Bitch who the fuck else would it be?" She snapped, daring her sister to try and block her escape.

"Will you give this to Eddie?" The whore replied. "Whenever you see him?"

"Mine too?"

"Yeah, me too, Tilly. I'll give him whatever else I make later tonight."

The lump of green bills grew large over Tilly's palm. More than two hundred dollars of Eddie's rightful bread. And why not? She was his bottom bitch after all.

Memories of the sunshine carried her thoughts as the ill gotten gains floated like a cloud in her hand.

She knew that there would be no escaping the man who owned her body. His reach had grown far too long for her to outrun.

But with two hundred dollars in her possession she could at least find her way through the night.

That if she stayed in motion she could evade punishment long enough to satisfy her joys and see the sun rise one last time. To feel God's voice touch her skin, and make peace in the event of her having to vacate the earth.

The whores before her seemed almost able to read her thoughts. They stood staring, waiting for her to finally break character, but she refused to give them the satisfaction.

"Bye bitches", she announced with a snap of her fingers, stepping out into the cold night with nothing more than the click of her heels in tow.

Tilly rested her head against the pane glass window, staring closely at the night while the 210 barreled north up Crenshaw. She made no attempt to hide her breasts or thighs from the ogling teenagers a few seats up. The truth was she didn't want to.

She was fully aware of how enticing her body could be.

That her stomach refused to fold no matter her posture. That her ass made even the thin steel bus seats as comfortable as a lounge chair. That her skin remained perfectly smooth even in the face of debilitating stress and a shit diet. She had always been blessed with the power of beauty, and she reveled in that power any chance she got.

"What y'all lookin' at?" She hollered to the two boys, who clearly had as little control over the eyes in their heads as they did the dicks in their pants.

"You, gorgeous", one piped.

"Gorgeous? Boy, ain't you too young to be callin' out girls on the bus? I know y'all or sum'?"

"I'm Demetrius", he stated proudly.

"Ronnie." The second boy followed.

"Oh. Well, hi Ronnie. And hi Demetrius."

"I see you around the neighborhood sometimes", Demetrius explained. "What's your name?"

"Angela," she replied with a much needed spark of amusement. Tilly could rarely pass on the opportunity to become someone outside herself.

"Are you a hoe, Angela?" Ronnie blurted out.

"Man, shut up!" Demetrius shoved.

Tilly dropped her jaw in feigned offense. "So that's why y'all been over there starin' at me? Cuz you think I'm some kinda hoe?"

"Not me", Demetrius covered. "I just think you're pretty."

"Aww, thank you", she said with a smile.

The boys struggled with their thoughts as they searched for some quip or question that might keep the conversation in play.

Tilly waited patiently in hopes that they could figure things out. As clumsy as the two had been, the chance to play in their reality was a much welcomed alternative to that of her own.

Without the tingle of a good distraction she could feel the rumble of Eddie's voice creeping into her ear.

'Bitch. Where the fuck you even 'bout to go, huh? Ya' really think ya' gonna be safe on the north side? That them crackers ain't fit'na see exactly what the fuck you iz? Even these little punks had yo' ass figured out.'

"How old are you", Demetrius finally gathered.

"I know I'm not supposed to ask, but…"

"Well why you think you can't ask?"

"It's what my mama tells me."

"Oh. Well yeah I guess. But that's just cuz your mamma's old, sweetheart. It's fine if the girl's still young and pretty like me. I'm nineteen", she beamed. At least that much was true.

"I'm sixteen." Demetrius rushed in an obvious lie"

"Really?" She hinted knowingly. "You don't look it. People must tell you you got a baby face all the time."

"Yeah. Sometimes", the boy played, keeping the moment as cool as he possibly could.

"And the baby body to go with it?" Tilly pointed out.

She fought back her giddiness as Ronnie turned to his friend with a face full of worry. Being turned down by a girl was one thing, but public humiliation had a way of following boys well into manhood, and a man still on to his grave.

Tilly began to wonder why she'd ever said such a thing in the first place. She had no intention of being cruel, lest she fill the world with more fools like the ones that frequented the Bougie Squirrel. As good as it felt being able to control a persons mind she couldn't bare to be responsible for any heartache. Not like Eddie.

"I'm only joking Demetrius", she assured. "You're very handsome."

The boy perked up with a rejuvenated smile aimed square in the direction of his pessimistic friend. In an attempt to right her wrong, Tilly had unwittingly provided the inspiration he needed to press forward.

He slid smoothly into the seat beside her. An all too familiar stride in his movement.

"So you like my body, huh?"

She fell into laughter, the good kind now.

"Oh-whee, honey. You have no idea how much I needed that."

"Happy to help." he voiced with manufactured depth, laboring to remove every inch of space between he and the woman he now adored.

In their newfound closeness, Tilly's eyes were introduced to a family of bruises and scars that had made a home around Demetrius' neck and forearms. For the first time she considered the time of night, and the fact that the boys were riding the bus all alone.

This one may have been lying about his age, but he had fair cause to believe himself more than a child. The same cause Tilly had when she and Eddie first began to pursue sex.

She knew better, of course, than to share this with him.

"You're awful close to me", she cautioned.

"Am I?" He teased.

"Tell me the truth. How old are you? Really?"

"Old enough for you to show me something."

"Ha! I doubt that. Besides, what would your mama think?"

Demetrius slid his gaze to every corner of the bus as if to say *I don't see her here to find out.*

Tilly's eyes rolled genuinely in response. He had succeeded in convincing her that he was not some innocent child, but it did nothing to help his case. She wasn't attracted to kids and was definitely in no mood to be seriously flirted with.

'Well ain't this about a mothafuckin' bitch', Eddie's voice resurfaced. *'You could'a did all this back at the Motel. C'mon baby. Let me show ya' the right way. You know yo' ass need me. You know—'*

"Young lady!" A voice called from the back of the bus. Tilly turned to find an elderly woman aiming a face full of judgement in her direction. "You know good 'n well you don't got no business wit' that boy", the woman croaked.

"Go on and leave him be"

"Excuse you?" Tilly fired back.

"I know who you are", the woman told. "Young man if you got any kinda sense you'll get away from that girl right now. Ain't nothin' good gonna come from dealin' wit' her."

"Uh-uh!" Tilly defended. "First of all you don't know shit about me, cuz I damn sure don't know who the hell you are."

"Young man", the woman urged, ignoring Tilly's assault. "You old enough to know right from wrong on ya' own. I done warned you about that girl already. If you got a mamma or daddy to think of, now's the time. Don't get yo'self wrapped up in no trouble on this bus."

Tilly turned to Demetrius, shocked to find him avoiding eye contact, clearly struggling with the weight of the old woman's words. How could he be so quick to second guess their friendship? She certainly didn't mean him any harm.

"I can see you's a good boy", the old woman coaxed. "And that girl right there can't do nothin' but put a burden on yo' head that you do not want."

Tilly cut her eyes narrow in the old woman's direction as she lifted her left foot and pressed its heel beside her thigh on the seat. She could feel Demetrius' eyes beam at the sight of her pink cotton panties, which had become visible as a result.

With the woman locked firmly in her sights, Tilly hung out her tongue and ran a finger slowly across it, then pulled the crotch of her panties aside, exposing her clean shaven vagina underneath.

Demetrius' jaw all but fell to the ground. Ronnie's head nearly hit the roof as he shot to his feet along with two other men on the bus in search of a better view.

Tilly never lifted her gaze from the old woman, whose only remaining comebacks were a slow shaking head and burdening scowl.

From the corner of her eye, she could see Demetrius'

hand inching slowly toward her naked parts. She allowed him another second of hope before slapping it away, then quickly correcting her skirt and returning her foot to the ground.

"Fuck that old bitch", she said to the still shocked adolescent beside her.

Tilly had only visited the north side on two occasions. Once in high school during she and her mother's brief pitstop on their way to the Valley. The other when Eddie took her shopping for her work costumes. The latter is how she'd first discovered Melrose.

It wasn't that she necessarily enjoyed the neighborhood, or the brand of white folks who shopped and played in its stores. After all, what was there to be enjoyed in a race of people who got by on throwing stones and hiding hands?

Then of course there were all the kinky intimates their men indulged in the secrecy of hotel beds. At this point it had become an act of labor to even take them seriously.

But in spite of the wall between them, the white folks that congregated on Melrose still managed to give Tilly hope. Not hope, of course, in their ability to be good people. But by the way they sought to combat the sinful nature to which they were born. An act of rebellion that, shockingly, always led them to embrace those cultures they would otherwise be responsible for tearing down.

Whether it was the men dressed in leathers and Mohawks like Indian warriors, or women piercing their faces and dyeing their hair like African tribes, somewhere in the DNA of these counter culture geeks lived the spirit of those humans who ought have been. They beamed with a kind of double sided truth, which, for some reason, brought great comfort to Tilly's spirit.

And so it was Melrose, with its bubbling storefronts and its down played eateries, and ad-hoc art houses, where she decided to part ways with the bus. An on the fly substitute for South Central, where she would hide out from Eddie and his inevitable persecution. To do this, however, she would first need to address the issue of her wardrobe.

There was no shortage of women in leather skirts and high heels lining the curbs that night, but none of them were built quite like Tilly. Tilly, whose body was an energy onto itself.

She settled on a store with big block letters that spelled the curious title "NEO80" over its front. There she bought herself a glittering pair of orange leather pants with a jacket made of the same style, only darker in shade and with black, thunderbolt shaped embroideries surrounding the collar.

She loved the way the suit made her look. Like a hip, but business minded woman, due to ride off in her powerful sleek sports car at any moment.

Now who gon' wanna fuck you in somethin' like that? She pictured Eddie saying.

A pitiful young saleswoman with pink and pale skin had been going on about how, on Tilly, the outfit reminded her of Cleopatra Jones, only more pretty to be sure.

This kind of covert hate-filled compliment was common among white women, who loved to try and downplay her beauty with nonsensical comparisons. It was as if to say 'your pretty goes over there, in the colored section.'

She fantasized for a moment about how easy it would be to make a stomping post of the little girl, with hands or words just the same. But in the midst of her daydream Tilly was quickly reminded of the piercing guilt she'd had to overcome after insulting Demetrius. That, and how when it came to women, experience had already taught her there was no need to exact revenge.

Nothing changed the fact that she was more beautiful than the tiny saleswoman could ever hope to be. Not to mention that while Tilly was out freely enjoying herself and spending money, the saleswoman was very much tethered and bound to work. More specifically, work for her.

"Do you mind folding this outfit I came with?" She told the girl with an irresistible warmth. "I just know you'll do it better than I could, girl. I can't fold worth a damn."

She smiled wide watching the woman swallow her own self hatred. Strangely satisfied to see it in the eyes of someone else for a change.

"Yeah girl, go ahead and put that in a bag for me too. You really think I look like Cleopatra?" She twirled and posed to show off all the features she knew the woman secretly envied. Tussling the fluff of her hair and rubbing carelessly about her curves.

It was fortunate for the tiny salesgirl, that while Tilly did quite literally have all night, she did not have all night for her. Not with Eddie's money burning a hole in her pocket, and not with the culmination of hours stirring a growl in her belly.

In what felt like no time at all, the pink and white servant had already melted into a dry powder of memories, as the marble red booth at Johnny Rocket's found Tilly in a four way wrestling match with a basket of fries, double cheeseburger, and large shake.

A fit of laughter sprung loose when she thought of how she must have looked. Specifically when compared to her earlier self notion of the sharp business woman.

But all that mattered to Tilly was that she was having fun. She was still over a hundred dollars strong with roughly six hours to kill before the sun rose, and was looking forward feeling God's voice for the first time in months.

As desperate as she'd been to get away from Eddie, she couldn't help but think on how much, under different circumstances, he might admire the night she was having. A night filled with pure fearlessness, which she knew him to respect above all else, save of course his precious money.

Against her better judgment, she allowed visions of Eddie and the sunshine to swirl together forming memories in her mind.

"When I's little", he'd told her on the day of the mushrooms, "I used ta' lay back on a school bench same way we doin' this grass right now. And I would lay there, and I'd stare up into them clouds and that sky for a good while. I mean 'long as I could 'til it started feelin' like that big blue sky was just a lazy river, and I was floatin' right 'round with the puffs.

"And I'd lay there. And I'd keep my eyes open wide as I could... then roll on over and fall straight to the ground.

"Oooo-wee!" He'd said with reclaimed excitement. "When I tell ya' my body swore it'd just jumped from the tallest buildin' in the world..! But not one of them falls ever took even a second." She remembered the way he laughed at the idea. As if it were something that hadn't truly belonged to him, but one lifted from the side of a road on his way to entertain her. "That's how I got my confidence up, ya know? I'd take that fall over and over again til one day I realized my fear wasn't no smarter than a dog after it's own tail. It ain't have a plan, or even good sense to make outta what it was wantin'. Just out here runnin' 'round jonsin' for the next fix."

Eddie's words spread and draped themselves over Tilly's shoulders. Warmth and comfort at long last finding her in the dreary night. Even with all he'd put her through somehow their memories still felt like home.

For a moment she had forgotten herself, lost somewhere between her physical body and the soft mold of her dream. But her eyes could not in good conscience allow her to drift.

With his long perfect legs, and his handsomely trimmed afro, and his enigmatic face, Tilly watched frozen as Eddie stalked past the window of Johnny Rockets.

How did he find me? she thought. *No one knows another person that well.*

Bolted by terror, she clung to the fork in her hand, waiting to see if he would double back and find her.

She thought for a moment that she might die from the adrenaline, until a pack of stray geeks invited themselves to her booth.

"Hey girl? What's shakin'?" A girl-geek lead.

Tilly put down her fork, grabbing hold of the rumble in her gut to spray a deep belch across their faces. She was not surprised by the eruption of cheers and high-fives that came in response. This batch was easy to read.

"Alright!" one hollered.

The geeks proceeded to introduce themselves and make pleasantries as Tilly measured the loaded window behind them. She could not be bothered to reciprocate or remember names. The pack had already been identified in her mind as Mullet, Mustache, Nose Ring, Nipple Ring, Brown Vest, and Wallet Chain, and she knew full well that as friendly as they were attempting to be, friendship was not why they'd chosen to visit.

It is an odd thing to witness the way white folks respond to the feeling of being seen by blacks. The hoops they jump to correct opinions that they themselves decide to project on dark skin. In this case, the freaks were eager to convince Tilly that they were not as evil as their pigments would suggest, but also, they wanted to staple this notion to her forehead and parade her around as proof of such to the other whites in attendance.

Tilly remained unmoved by the exhibition. She knew that the gusto with which they paraded their self sacrifice would be accompanied by the singular benefit of submission. The desire to give as a form of receiving.

She smiled her slightest smiles, and nodded only half nods, but was sure to indulge fully those judgmental stares from the surrounding whites. Both the geeks success and their self worth hung on their ability to recruit her in the presence of these silent hecklers. It was vital that they not feel the cool breeze of victory until she was given what she truly wanted.

"Y'all live around here?" Tilly asked with a twinge of

annoyance.

"I do", Nipple Ring responded. "It's a quick walk if you wanna get into a little peace pipe action?"

"No thanks", she fired quickly. Any drug that was not a fungus was the last thing on Tilly's mind. "Y'all got cigarettes?"

The geeks walked with their heads held high. Newly minted grace and confidence shining through their movement as Tilly's black body stepped beside them toward the double glass exit.

She kept her chin to her chest, unable to convince herself that their numbers would ensure safety, but knew that if they did happen to land in Eddie's view, the males would at least be dumb enough to try and stop him.

She hunched and hid as the night air once again ran over her body. The Geeks continued their smalltalk and lit their sticks of cancer as she bore relief with every turn of her neck. There was no sign of Eddie.

"So, Angela", one started. "Where you from?"

But Tilly was already in the wind.

"Thanks for the smoke", she shot as she tossed the half lit stick and shuffled down the corridor of lifeless storefronts. Metal gates and pad locks refusing her refuge at every turn.

Did he follow me here? She thought. *I didn't see him when I left the motel.*

The plastic store bag curled and rustled against her leg as her feet clapped hurriedly down the sidewalk. She felt vulnerable and exposed under the taunting glow of neon lights.

"Fuck, fuck, fuck", she told herself as she turned down a dimly lit side street.

She couldn't be sure of whether the shadows would aid or sabotage her efforts to escape, but in the moment the cocoon of darkness felt right.

See that? Eddie's voice taunted from the back of her

mind. *Ya' runnin' cuz you know you wrong. How many times I got to tell ya' it ain't no you wit'out me? How much of my patience you gon' try wit' this Tom and Jerry bullshit? I done had 'bout enough of you fuckin' 'round. This time I'm puttin' yo' ass down for good.*

"Someone's in a hurry."

Tilly halted her walk at the deep and soothing sound that rang from across the street. She knew before her eyes confirmed that its speaker was black, and could all but taste the urge of demand rumbling in his throat.

She studied the composition that now stood before her. A man in a suit, clean and tailored, but still somehow incapable of concealing the chiseled structure that lay beneath.

His sturdy frame pressed heavily against a well shone Lincoln, whose black paint gleamed sharp in the night just like the skin of its owner.

"I can give you a ride if you need to be somewhere."

Tilly put on her best impression of a woman wrestling with doubt, allowing a somewhat respectable number of seconds to pass before responding with a crass and trite 'How much?' in the same condescending tone that had afflicted her so many times before.

"Depends on where you goin'", he said without flinching.

"I never been to a hotel before. A nice one, I mean."

With an easy nod he released the car from the weight of his shoulders and moved to open its rear door. Before climbing inside Tilly hurried to shed the plastic shopping bag that still carried her work costume. *This ain't that*, she assured herself.

The car's interior was all business. Mints and beverages and reading materials strategically placed about her large leather seat. A small laminate card perched eagerly in the crease of her door explaining clearly what was free and what was not as her driver held his stoic gaze to the road ahead. But the air between them was charged with intimacy.

Tilly's body still rang with adrenaline from the sight of her stalker, and the unassuming strength of the man before her felt like a lighting rod, begging to be struck by all that bubbled inside.

"You gonna tell me your name?" She pressed.

"Charles", he offered sparingly. "And you are?"

"Tilly."

"It's late out here Tilly. Thought I was done for the night."

"Me too."

She set the words before him with a whimper of brokenness, inviting them to be cradled and soothed by the unspoken wisdom a man like this was bound to possess. But her chauffeur was silent.

"Where're you takin' me?"

"The Biltmore. You'll like it there. Pretty girl like you'll fit right in."

It was all she could do not to blush at the idea. She imagined herself being whisked to some royal ball with fluffy corsets and bell shaped dresses, and pinned up hair-dos to the point she became nervous at the thought of being under dressed.

"Do you like my outfit", she whispered, caressing the leather about her torso, daring him to meet her helpless eyes in the rearview. To his credit her driver did what he could to resist, but Tilly had long decided that Charles was going to get what she had to give.

There were men with morality strong enough to resist a sure thing, but to resist a thing that would be surely good ventured into the realm of foolishness.

Their first touch happened at the valet, when she all but dove into his path, so that the only way to avoid collision was by stiffening his hand against the small of her back. This, followed by a well timed spin that brushed the tips of her breasts across his shoulder, and a quiet 'excuse me' that allowed the softness of her words to massage his neck and chin.

An agreement was soon made that her lack of experience in the ways of hotel etiquette would require both guidance and company, for which no better suitor than Charles could possibly be found.

Their first drink came with a click of crystal over smooth piano, and a conversation that was light but not void of meaning. They talked for hours about all of the things that made them happy, and none of the things that didn't.

Charles proved to be a man who flirted with looks and touch, so that even if he said that water was wet, it somehow felt like an invitation to become undressed.

Their first kiss melted and rolled its way from the lobby, to the elevator, to the hall, and only stopped when they accepted the impossibility of unlocking her room door in such a state.

He was first to put his mouth below her waist. She was first to be on top and prove her nature.

Every first was drown in her mind like the names of lovers in wet cement. This was her first time making love. Her first time being honored and taught and chosen and given to in a way that made her feel free.

But when she came it was not the same as with Eddie.

"Watch out for him", she whispered. Falling asleep in Charles' arms.

"Who?" He asked.

"He won't let me feel the sun. You have to be gone when it comes up."

Charles thought to press deeper, but her breath drifted into sleep, and the thought of waking her broke his heart into pieces. There was no need to ruin things by trying to make more out of it.

So he slid out of bed and redressed in his uniform and went back into the world in search of his next fare.

A naked body laid in bed when the sun rose. It carried the same shape and texture and history as Tilly's, but it was no longer hers.

It rose with a frown of discontentment and rushed for the remaining money in her outfit pants.

"Gat damnit!" A voice sprang from the bodies throat, as it hurled less than twenty dollars to the pillow and stormed to the bathroom mirror.

The body stared into the glass, and from the glass found Eddie staring back in return.

"Did you enjoy yo'self, bitch? Spendin' up all my gat damn money on that trick! You better pray I don't run into his ass again, cuz if I do I'll cut is fuckin' throat."

A tear dripped from the body's eye, begging its reflection to stop.

"You'd better not cry, bitch I warned ya'! All you had to do was gimmie the time of day, but you just couldn't make no more of it, huh? We'll now I'm in charge. I'm goin' to the track to see my hoes, and get my money, and the next time I let yo' ass out it'll be in a room full'a hard dicks."

"Agh!" The body screamed.

"Shut up!" The reflection yelled, as it forced the body to grab a pair of scissors and cut the hair from its crying head.

Eddie stepped out of the hotel with his perfect long legs and his handsomely trimmed afro and the face of a woman who had somehow forgotten her own beauty, as the sun washed over skin he once again possessed.

"God picked me, bitch" he said before storming back out into the world.

HELL
(or EXPERIMENTAL)

A MAN IN A HOUSE on a street in a town. The town lives on a planet, and the planet circles a star, and the star circles a star much larger than itself.

The reality needled his spirit. An incessant fire tickling his every thought.

The man in the house had no peace.

He suffered from eating disorders, sleeping disorders, anxieties and depressions.

He vomited often.

He did not enjoy the company of others.

He bubbled with rage when they asked what was wrong, and he broke down in tears when they did not understand his answer.

"This is not my house", he would say. "This is not my street and this is not my town. This is not my planet and those are not my stars."

They laughed.

He'd been abducted by aliens, and not even the aliens believed his story.

These creatures could not see that their skin was blue from sickness. They didn't know that their air was poison, or that their food would turn a real human's stomach.

Cannibalism at their dinner tables.

Orgies in the presence of their children.

In his real home, they'd be lowest among the beasts, and yet here they are God. Bringers of both plagues and miracles the like.

They intersect his life in the form of merchants, prophets, beggars, soldiers, teachers, foes, bedmates, and empathizers.

And the empathy tortures him. The comfort of kindness that threatens to remove his needle and extinguish his fire. To convince him that these creatures somehow reflect what he is. Are somehow human.

They are not.

And so as the man sits awake in the house that isn't his — listening close for the voice of the devil in his echoing alarm— his soul's only peace dangles on the hope of making it back home. Back to truth. Back to freedom.

"SHYAAAHHTTTAHUUUUP!"

He does this. Screaming with his physical body the way his muffled spirit cannot.

He likes to punch hard on the alarm clock until his knuckles raw. Knowing it isn't enough to quiet the piercing ring. He knows that the only escape from it, and all the other tortures, is to play their game.

Press the button, put on the clothes, and go to work.

In the streets he sees them. Ghoulish looking things with goat legs and devil faces. Walking with limps and heavy shoulders as they impersonate a civil society.

Are these the demons of classic paintings? Did Da Vinci and Van Gough spend time in this mad place? Are they the reason the creatures feign humanity?

He feels them watching, judging, studying, though they pretend not to notice him.

The man is always exposed. Always alone.

"Delroy!" a voice howls. "I can't find my 3/4 socket anywhere. Mind if I borrow yours?"

This creature calls itself Chad. Chad reeks of sulfur and is always showing the empty gum holes that once held its teeth. This pisses Delroy off.

He grabs the socket sitting atop his toolbox and shoves it into his pocket. Then snaps and hisses to scare the shit out of Chad.

"Jesus— Christ man! Forget it. I'll ask Paco."

Delroy lets himself breathe. He'll never get used to the sight of their hideous bodies. The fleshy gills where their throats should be.

The creatures don't see with their eyes.

Do they know they're outside? he wonders.

Do they know that fire shoots from the ground? Do they make the fires?

There would be no way for Delroy to see at this time of night without them.

He heaves hard in his attempt to loosen an old bolt. Back tight. Hands stinging from the heat. This work exhaust him.

Good.

Exhaustion forges truth within his mind. The great ballroom where misery drags joy across the dance floor. It was here that he was first able to see God's complicity in the creatures' plan. That he could only be worked to death because he was created with the desire to fulfill purpose. That God, having created such a magnificent passion, then failing to protect it, made him low hanging fruit for the jaws of evil.

God.

Aliens.

Demons.

Delroy.

He would never understand.

DAD DID WHAT DADS DO when things that needed doing had to get done. When the day demanded dutiful diligence the domestically downtrodden decided to drink.

Gulp, gulp, gulp, gulp.

Damn.

Dad had to dig deep to dedicate doting diction to his son Demetrius, who didn't display determination, or decisiveness, and definitely didn't demand desirability. Still, duty drove him to devise a direction for his son's development.

"Demetrius!" Dad decreed. "Downstairs! Double time!"

Demetrius drudged down donning a dull demeanor. Deliberately denying dad the dedication that would have delighted him.

"What did I do?" Demetrius droned.

"Do?" Dad demanded. "Ya' haven't done dick all day!"

Demetrius dubbed Dad's digs as deliberate denials to his dignity, which drove a drastic division into their daily dealings.

Gulp, gulp, gulp.

"Don't dick around you little delinquent." Dad doubled down. "I've decided to dedicate the day to your discipline. "

"Dedicate?" Demetrius dished. "Doesn't that distract from your drinking?"

"Do the decent thing and demonstrate some damn deference. The dishes are past due and the den's a downright disgrace. Dust the drapes, disinfect the dinette, deep clean the dog, and detail the Dodge."

"Detail the Dodge? Dad, didn't mom deal you these duties during dinner the other day?

"Don't debate me damnit!"

"Just do your own damn work and don't dump it on me, dummy."

"Dummy? Dimwit!"

"Douchebag!"

"Dead-weight!"

"Doo-doo brain!"

"How dare you defy my direction?"

"Direct deez nutz dickhead."

"Dickhead? Ya' done done it now."

Dad downed the last drop of his drink while dirty dragging Demetrius to the door.

"You don't deserve my dedication", he denounced. "You're a damn disaster!"

"I hope you die!" Demetrius drawled.

Without deliberation, Dad dropped Demetrius down on the doorstep, driving the door shut as Demetrius dove desperately for his dockers.

DOOMF!

A done deal. The deathless divide of Dad and Demetrius forever drawn. A devotion derailed by the dastard deed. A darkness dedicated to the dampening of any day that drums up depictions of the word...

— Dad

CHAUNCEY WAS IN LOVE

CHAUNCEY was in love... but it didn't matter.

A woman stood before him with skin that glowed and hair that flowed. Eyes so deep he wanted to strip down and go swimming. Lips he could live in.

Chauncey was in love.

With a smile. With a touch. With the smell of the air around her.

How did she do it? He wondered. To make her flaws feel so perfectly necessary? To have a voice that sang when it whispered?

She shimmered in her sundress. A body full of hope. He held her. Kissed her. Caressed. Undressed. She made herself belong to him, from the arch in her back to the song in her heart.

But it didn't matter.

Chauncey had a wife. Not someone who loved him, but had invested. Someone with whom he shared responsibility. A home.

He knew the physical act performed on this night was no betrayal. Between he and his investor there was nothing physical left to betray.

The only true sin would be to lie in bed with his lover. To hold her in his arms and close his eyes. To wake in the morning and live a life that was new. Only then would he have betrayed the time and sacrifice of the woman waiting at home. Only then would he have transgressed beyond his nature.

Chauncey was in love... but it didn't matter.

It was 11:53 when he walked through the door, seven minutes to midnight, and although he'd done his part to preserve the space he was entering, his home felt like so much less than a worthwhile reward.

How? He thought. How in the world could *this* be the life he had chosen? Who in their right mind would chose to live in a state of perpetual longing?

To...

To...

There was no point. There was no moment to be identified as the inception of this existence. No time of death for the youth and joy that once filled his heart.

He allowed himself a breath, long and deep, dusting off his dwindling pride as he waited silently and out of sight. Watching from across the dark room as colors danced over his wife's body. Her face fixed on the glowing screen mounted to the thin wall between them. Shafts of younger, more beautiful women pulsing over her fleshy silhouette — an insult to his manhood.

Still, it made him happy to see her happy. Comfortable and protected. She smiled when he sat down beside her.

"What's this?" He asked with routine curiosity.

"A documentary. It's about a woman who catches her husband cheating, so she hired a guy to cut off his balls."

"Jesus. Couldn't she have just divorced him?"

"Then she'd be giving him what he wanted."

"Yeah but she wouldn't have to go to jail. Why ruin

her own life just to get back at him?"

"Til death do us part, baby."

He sits with this. Unsure what to make of his wife's opinion.

No man falls in love with loyalty, or admiration, or humor, or common interest. No woman for that matter either. The first thing anyone seeks in this world is validation. After that the rest are only trinkets.

Cruelly, Chauncey's wife had long forfeited her ability to validate him. Letting herself become fat and unsexual. She made no effort to dress up, or display longing, or talk nice, or revere him as her greatest source of pleasure. As if she deemed it noble to protest such acts after having secured the position of an honorable wife.

'Wife', he thought. The title meant more to her than he ever would. For him she couldn't find the strength to lift a single finger, but for that title she had already ended his life.

The only reason I'm with you is because there was a time when I hated myself. I thought that if I could make something of loving you then it would help me past that hate, but it didn't. In the end our relationship only exposed and deepened the ugly truth. These days I wake up ready to love myself again, but I can't do that with you reminding me to hate every time I see you.'

These were the words Chauncey spoke with every look, and every touch, and every bit of quiet he gave to his wife. But never once with his lips. Those would remain tightly sealed as he spent his years sitting beside her. Watching her watch her shows.

EFFIE

IF ANYONE was looking for Effie, she was in the living room. Not that she was hoping to be looked for. It just so happened that in the moment she recognized where she was, and, in this, took a great deal of pride.

In truth, Effie didn't even know the word 'living room'. How could she? The letter of the day was being shown for the fourth time on Sesame Street, and she still hadn't the foggiest idea of what to do about it.

Colors were what she recognized. Faces, voices, patterns, shapes, music, feelings, temperatures, and of course her mommy's milk. Matters that God had clarified to her personally in the womb.

These were the things that made up her life. Her world. And the time she spent in their orbit was always time well spent.

Well spent, that was, when the hard thing was not around. The hard thing that liked to drop sneaky doses of frustration and resentment into her still forming psyche. That sent her into uncontrollable fits it later adored. The adoration, of course, being just a different flavor of sneaky.

The hard thing stayed on Effie's mind even when it wasn't around — in her day dreams and her night ones. Partly because of the growing fear it watered before leaving, but also because she was still trying to figure out what exactly the thing was.

To define the hard thing as people would not have been quiet right. Although people is definitely where it lived. She didn't understand it's relationship to them, or why they let it hang around when it was clearly no good. Least of all could she determine why it seemed to be so specifically interested in her.

Whenever Effie was face to face with another person they were wonderful. Everyone seemed to be made of warm smiles and persistent joys that filled her spirit with all the best kinds of happy. She didn't need to know the word love to know that it was something she had in abundance… when people faced her.

But when play time dwindled and people move on to face one another, this was when the hard thing showed it's face.

As if Effie somehow became invisible without a steady supply of eye contact, people would start to behave themselves in ways that did not make any sense. Yelling, and crying, and setting fires to small sticks that they would breathe into their bodies. Little clouds that would float toward Effie, causing her to dizzy and cough.

People weren't the same when they looked away from her, and she wondered constantly if they knew. If they could feel the hard thing tying strings around their hands and heads. Dancing them around like an ugly puppet show just for her.

For hours on end the hard thing made her watch while the people who loved her did what it wanted, laughing in her face as she wordlessly struggled to warn them of what was happening.

Why hadn't God told her about this? Of all the things he'd made clear to her in the womb, why wouldn't he warn her about the hard thing? He couldn't have forgot. Could he?

It didn't matter. For now Effie was safe in the living room. There were no people, and no hard thing that came with them. She was free to fall in love with the one and only constant in her life… Television.

"But these rail at whatsoever things they know not: and what
they understand naturally, like the creatures without reason, in these
things they are destroyed.

"Woe unto them! For they went in the way of Cain, and ran
riotously in the error of Balaam for hire, and perished in the
gainsaying of Kora.

"These are they who are hidden rocks in your love-feasts when
they feast with you, shepherds that without fear feed themselves; clouds
without water, carried along by winds; autumn trees without fruit,
twice dead, plucked up by the roots;"

— *The book of Jude*

Your Narrator, A Séance

There is a howl in the wind. The smell of wood, burned by fire, and blood sizzling against cast iron. Flakes of rust jabbed into pupils as eyelids get carved from quivering skulls. Men whimper with tears and coughs as the ache of regret drips from the same crack in what must now feel to them like the exact same soul — eyes flung open and forced to swallow sights that only the most seasoned of torturers could imagine…

You've made it.

Oh of course I knew you would. Still, I must admit how it warms me to have you along, trusted reader. Trusted, after all, for your endurance in the art of sadism. That even after the murder, torture, castration, and even child abuse, you stayed. Page after page, you wet your mouth with the blood of the afflicted. Developing your own taste for the madness.

Now that you're here with me, allowing my thoughts to be yours, I wonder. Do you realize how they will never leave? That you and I have become one — for this, and all of the moments that haunt your memory until the day you die?

This time is so special, is it not?

Right now it is night. The moon is full. You and I are outside, seated in the courtyard of our beloved madhouse, surrounded by several dozen of our fellow inmates.

This includes Joseph and Kevin, of course. The tall man in all his quietude. Demetrius, who has grown to be a fine killer. Eddie, the schizophrenic pimp. All are here. All at least, that reside in the reality you know.

You have grown to love us, haven't you? To empathize and admire our brutish deeds? Good. Because you ain't seen nothing yet…

"No, please! I have children. And— and I'll do whatever you want if you just please… please don't do this to me! I only did what they asked. It's a fucking job! Please!"

You may or may not have inferred, but the guards are no longer in command of our facilities. At present, many of them are hogtied and bound. Others have had their throats cut and are bleeding into buckets to fulfill the needs of tonight's rituals.

And yes. Lest I forget, I do believe it's high time to fill in a few gaps.

Give me a moment…

What's that Tilly? You want to know what I'm writing? Well an account of lord Lucifer's return, no doubt. Yes it will be quite glorious, I'm sure. Will Eddie be joining us? Well there's no need to get nasty about it. I assumed the two of you could take turns. Fine fine, then. I'll be seeing you. Goodbye now.

Pardon me trusted reader but I guess we'll be scratching Edward's name off the list for this evening. It really is too bad. He's a far better time than the girl if you ask me.

But no matter. For outside of our much anticipated guest of honor, you are the only participant who matters tonight. The kindred soul who meets us at the other end of space and time, extending our lives and the life of tonight's evocation.

You see, trusted reader, the madness is made up of much worthier stuff than a stomach for the grotesque or a penchant for violence, but verily, it is a spirit, both ethereal and physical in its nature. A spirit so violently pure that those who succumb to its will may accomplish things which todays humans readily dismiss as impossible.

Like Adam and Eve after their first bite of fruit, you and I now stand privy to the origins of man, the true shape of hell, the secret to alternate realities, and what it really means for a man, women, or child to lose their very minds.

But beneath our great triumph lies a confession. One I have held out of necessity and not malice — though the malice has left me tickled at times.

To clarify, on the subject of tonight's carnage, you, trusted reader, will be playing a far greater role than passive benefactor.

It is finally safe to reveal that the nature of stories you have thus far consumed were in fact commissioned by Kevin and Joseph, to be recounted in such a way that, without realizing it, would imprint thoughts of the devil onto your hapless mind. A kind of forced hypnosis, administered to illicit both a focus and energy that could be drawn upon during tonight's channeling.

It was a truly fiendish plot to be sure. But as I've already confessed the devil does very little to inspire me. And being a man driven solely by the compulsion of inspiration, it only makes sense that I would opt not to honor my pact with the prophets, and instead plant a more suitable subject in the depths of your subconscious. One I have pursued for a good while, but have yet to be able to pin down.

Thus the villain of my tales has been made the very same one that plagues your daily life.

And tonight, under the full moon and stars, with the blood of the guards, and the wisdom of the prophets, and the madness in your very own heart, you and I will be summoning God.

No, you have not misread me. For who with the mind to profit would waste the knowledge of eternity on an exiled child when the mighty father himself could be had?

This, my wretched workmate, is true ambition.

But what's that you say? Blasphemy? Quite the contrary. For whenever two or more are gathered in his name he who knows all has promised to be present. My only intention is to hold the deity to his word.

Which brings us at long last to the nitty gritty. As I look around I see all of the usual elements at play. Pentagrams made of blood and sand. Raw eggs, dead chickens, a caldron pot, candles, men in robes, and one very naked Tilly, covered in just about all the blood she can stand. I guess it would have been a bit awkward for Eddie to have joined us after all, wouldn't it?

But the tastiest detail is this. That there is even a 'double' double cross on top of my own.

It just so happens that the true intention of our prophets has been not to free the devil, but rather to imprison the fallen son, rendering him to their own mercy.

It seems that two additional years of life lived exclusively in a madhouse were not good enough terms to elicit their loyalty.

This now means that when the chants are chanted, and the offerings are offered, and the summoning brings forth the summoned, we will not only have the almighty Yahweh in our presence, but at our feet.

Do not play coy with me now trusted reader. I know you want answers. I can feel your burning need for restitution, reciprocity, and dare I suggest, a drop of revenge? Yes. Think hard of the ones that have maimed you. Every foe he chose to be worthier than thou in the presence of victory. Every debilitating flaw he's stitched to your soul to be mocked throughout time.

Think hard of Demetrius, and Effie, and Christopher, and Joshua.

Think of them and know who he is. Who did the prophets discover to be the architect of hell? Who counts your sin twice as often as your courage?

Admit it. He is not pure, or loving, or generous with his blessings. He is exactly as you are, and the only thing that sets him apart is the upper hand. But tonight, the upper hand belongs to us. We will shape the world and our reality to be as we see fit! Without judgment! And without gatekeeping! Fasten your intentions reader! The prophet Joseph speaks!

THINGS THEY KNOW NOT

CHAPTER 1

1 And so insanity was the plague that corrupted the lives of men.

2 For an entire world was gifted unto he who would cast out his own pleasure for ambition.

3 That somehow the sun was no longer enough, and corruption was his culture.

4 Nothing is impossible for the Lord our God, who grants all reward, and stops all suffering. But even this favor can not quell the thirst of man, for he seeks not God's blessing, but to become God himself.

5 What began with Adam and his wife in the garden had engulfed the earth during the times of Enoch. And at the very moment that the land was washed clean, Noah scandalized his son, and the cycle was born anew.

6 Madness.

7 To know both more and less than what is required for one's survival. To hold the infinite scope of reality in their gaze only to realize that the gaze is no match for what it sees.

CHAPTER 2

1 "It's you." The man cried with a deep and cathartic breath. "I can't believe it, it's— It worked!"

2 It did not work.

3 God did *not* stand naked in the circle of blood and sand that had been prepared for him. Nor did he wear a look of earnest confusion at the spectacle of death and carnage that surrounded it. Never the less, this is what the man managed to see.

4 In fairness to God, He also did not speak to Abraham in a tent. Or count talisman with Moses on mount Sinai. Or appear before Isaiah on a throne.

5 But He watched them all think He did.

6 "You... You really..." The man's face began to shrew. "You motherfucka!"

7 God's eyes are not eyes. All that ever has or will exist cannot begin to fill the scope of his vision.

8 God's words are not words, but the very movement of the universe is a mere octave in his voice.

9 To speak directly with man is to ruin him, and so the same to give him free rein on the infinite plain of all that is.

10 But the infinite was also the key to life.

11 So that thoughts and emotions, and matter and time are but pieces of the eternal, passing through the living creatures that anchor

it to its own existence, and within those pieces are hidden windows to the abyss of all.

12 "Oh I got yo' ass now. You hear me? I got you now, you bitch ass nigga!"

13 And behold, a window became open, and all of this is what the man learned when, for a brief moment, he was able to touch God.

14 "Look at me! Look at this fuckin' shit!"

15 The man rang his forearm in the face of his vision, and the vision noticed how the forearm stopped at a bleeding wrist, and how the bleeding wrist was impaled with a pencil, which the man planned on using to take account of his meeting with the Lord.

16 "Why the fuck you let me do this, huh? All of it? This whole damn time. Where the fuck was you?!"

17 In the grand scheme of things God had been simultaneously in every Planck of infinity throughout all of time, both before and after existence. But in relation to the man, he was right beside him. Just as he was right beside Joe.

18 "I'm sorry! I am so fuckin' sorry!" Joe wept openly at the feet of his own incarnation, which took the likeness of an elderly woman he and Kevin once saw on the deck of a rotting boat.

19 "I know ya' was there to warn us. I shoulda' listened, I know it. But we— we wasn't gon' do what that gray bastard told us, I promise we wasn't. We just didn't wanna go back. Oh please, please don't make us go back!"

20 God heard Joe and granted him forgiveness, knowing that Joe would sin again.

CHAPTER 3

1 And God also collected the soul of Chauncey, who was killed at a job he hated, trying to provide for a woman he did not love.

2 And in the same moment Demetrius felt the will of God, and opened the hand that held the knife that had done the killing. And when Demetrius looked upon that hand it was the hand of his earthly father.

3 Then his eyes met those of the man who had not hands, but touched the world with his anger alone. So he hid his eyes from the man and his hand from himself for fear that he would do what the man had done.

4 And God was pained by a pinch in his heart to bear witness on Tilly, for her shame was to be naked in his presence. This was the shame of Adam that had made man what he is, and caused God to hide himself in parables and visions from his own children.

5 And as God moved toward mercy to place peace in his daughter's heart he carried with him the vision of the man who then became strong with rage, and beat upon his vision with forearm and elbow and foot and knee.

6 And because his rage was strong and the vision came to be of the man's thoughts and emotion and will, those elements grew solid within the infinite and a single blow was felt by both God and the man, and the man became aware of all that was, and looked upon his brethren with new eyes that were filled with the awe and wonder of The Lord.

7 And he knew that the true God was beside him, and that those who carried the law of man were also close, and that by their hand he should soon die.

8 But verily, the man became wise with knowledge that not all was in vein. That the Lord had given him purpose and his purpose would be fulfilled in his last moments if he found the strength to write.

9 And when he looked down the man's hands had been made whole. And so it was that his last words filled the page, and that thou hast now read those words in their entirety.

10 And when the man was done he turned to God and said: "God? It's somethin' I wanna tell 'em too. I think it matters."

11 And God granted the man to write his words, and the words were these.

CHAPTER 4

1 "Look like the boys is here, y'all. I wanna thank ya' for hearin' my side of things, but I wanna warn ya' too. Don't look like I got much time cuz there they go breakin' down doors and throwin' tear gas and shit.

2 Kinda like when we first met, huh? 'Cept dis time don't look like ya' narrator's gonna make it. I already seen dem boys' gonna come in here and shoot for the head soon as they see me.

2 "But what I wanna warn ya' 'bout is dis. Everything that makes you you; well, ya' gotta know that's the only thing God gives ya'. So just find a way to listen to that, and nothin' else, ya get me? Cuz it's all bullshit. If it ain't come from Him it ain't worth —

THE DEFINITION OF INSANITY

Today I sought to know the truth
But truth said not today
I asked truth why
And it replied
Because you are insane
And parts of me
That are to be
Revealed for joy and progress
Will only loom
For men like you
In thoughts that feel like nonsense
I told truth no
This can't be so
I beg you reconsider
Truth crossed its arms
And with a yawn
Said plus you are a ███
If in your life
You push and fight
And somehow come to grow
And hold me near
For years and years
You still would never know
Too many lives
are built on lies
Just special made for you
So as you grow
And build your own
You'll always be confused
Well in this case I'll never build
And never yield
I threatened
Truth hung it's head
And sadly said
That there in lies your lesson

SOUTH CENTRAL

I

IF ONE were to chose two activities that best defined P Money they would undoubtedly be selling dope and fucking fat girls.

Few people could account for a time that he was not either in the midst or on his way to do one or the other.

In a vacuum, one might label these acts as trifling, but the hood appreciated P Money, for he kept them all grounded in truth.

Whenever a poser came around flaunting his nice car and clean clothes and trophy girl, the fiends and robbers all knew good and well that they were dealing with a mark.

No man true to the game could possibly have the time to acquire and maintain such goods. A quality dealer should have no obligations outside of selling dope and fucking fat girls.

II

Kimberly Smith does a lot of fucking. In response to this, a group of scientists have gathered to analyze the decline in her physical appearance, which seems to steepen with every new man she beds.

"You gotta think bro", a biochemist offered. "That shit is literally exchanging DNA. It warps the whole fuckin' structure of who you are as a human."

Then a behavioral therapist chimed in.

"Shit is emotional, dawg. "It's gon' be draining on her energy and happiness and femininity. All the shit that makes you attractive to a man."

"Nobody wanna be out wit' his girl worried about runnin' into the last nigga she fucked", said he of cognitive studies.

The scientists theorized, and hypothesized, and exchanged notes for the full duration of two blunts and a full bottle of Hennessy, but not one could come up with a single scenario in which they themselves wouldn't smash.

III

In the early days no one questioned Fish's pimping.

He kept a consistent rotation of hoes, always 4-5 deep, who lived with him in his mother's back house.

His best customers frequented multiple times a week, and stayed for hours on end, smoking his weed, fucking his hoes, and settling up with his bottom bitch Hazel before they left.

Hazel always ensured that the trap was clean and that Fish remained undisturbed by any troubles that arose due to business.

Fish in return kept Hazel as clean as possible with a respectable wardrobe and a right of refusal for low level jons.

In those days, Fish would brag how a bottom bitch's job was to take care of her man.

He since learned that the true objective of any bottom bitch is to break the will of her pimp and get him out of the game so that she may have him to herself.

Fish and Hazel still live in his mother's back house with their daughters ebony and maya. Neighbors often gossip over the young family and speculates as to whether or not Fish was ever a real pimp to begin with. But no one ever asks this about Hazel.

IV

"Hey, just so we clear homie I really don't give a fuck. I don't give a fuck and I don't wanna hear nobody's opinion 'bout what I got goin' on. Ya feel me? Matter fact the next nigga tryna offer me a opinion fit'na fuck around and get these hands, on God. I don't care if it's to tell me what he like for breakfast, he gettin five on his eye and I dare him to do summ about it."

"I did what I did because I could and because I felt like it. Motherfuckers wanna talk all this shit about how it look or what they don't like. You do it then, bitch ass nigga. Talkin all that fuckin shit. Gimme fifteen."

Corey had no intention of letting up. With the form of a well trained pimp he slapped ivory to wood, bouncing his six/five domino onto Rod's new coffee table.

"Aight, nigga. Relax", Rod warned. "Damn."

"Nigga fuck a relax, homie!" Corey fired between slugs of his old English. "Niggas need to learn how to mind they God damn business. Don't be over there pencil whippin me neither."

V

Xiomara is always happiest when her children spend time with her. This is not something that happens often.

Her son Caleb would much rather play out his sadistic murder fantasies via video games, and her daughter Crystal wore the passion of a politician when gossiping with her friends over the phone.

In truth, the only quality time she gets is when the power goes out in her house.

During these not infrequent blackouts she has made a

tradition of lighting her fireplace, pouring a glass of wine, and listening to her psychotic children ramble and argue for hours at a time.

To Xiomara these are the best days of her life. Every blackout she prays to God that neither of her kids will catch her by the fuse box.

Your Narrator; A Transcript

The following session took place prior to the tragic massacre at the Southern California State Asylum for the Criminally Insane. It was recovered in the office of Dr. John Seller who took his own life to avoid being sacrificed by his patients.

The subject of this interview is believed to be the leader of the cult that killed over thirty hospital employees, though journals recovered by the suspect deny this claim.

This transcript is being made public for educational purposes only...

C1:Ya' ever notice how the word therapist
   is just 'the rapist' wit'out a space?
T1:(Laughs) Good morning to you too,
   Joshua. How are you today?
C2:Ah, shit! Is it mornin'? Hey why y'all
   don't give us no windows in here?
   Thought you wanted to make
   motherfucka's less crazy?
T2:Well now that you mention it that's a
   pretty good point. I'll talk to someone
   about moving you to a room with a
   window.
C3:Fa' real? Say, that's alright man. Hey
   but 'long as I keep my same roommate,
   ya' hear? He's helpin' me out with a
   little project I got goin' on.
T3:That's great. Do you want to tell me
   about it?
C4:I can tell ya' some, yeah. See I
   decided to to a little writin' in my
   down time. But ya' know, no hands and
   all. So my main man Demetrius is
   helpin' me out.
T5:I'm glad to hear it. I think that's
   good for both of you, actually.
C5:Yeah, yeah. Ya' know we was buttin'
   heads a little at first, but turns out
   heavy D is my kinda people.
T6:What inspired you to take this on?
C6:Hell, talkin' to Joseph's crazy ass. I
   was out shootin' the shit with him and
   Kevin and they hipped me to this idea
   that was pretty wild. So I said fuck

it, ya'know? Why not put this thang on
    paper?
T7:And what was the idea?
C7:See that I can't tell ya'. But I know I
    wanna do it in the style of like a Mary
    Shelly, Charles Dickens, Jayne Eyre…
T8:Really? I didn't think you'd be a fan
    of theirs.
C8:Shit yeah. Them's the original crazy
    niggas. Suicide, rape, murder, lies.
    I'm just payin' a little homage.
T9:Mm-hm. You know you've been talking a
    lot about spending time with Kevin and
    Joe and I wonder—
C9:Joseph! Joseph, man. C'mon now, put
    some respect on that man's name.
T10:   Joseph, of course, yes. I wanted to
    ask if you think that has anything to
    do with their relationship? How close
    the two of them are and maybe it
    reminds you sometimes of Christopher?

No response.

T11:   Joshua?
C10:   Why you gotta bring that shit up? I
    told you I don't wanna talk about it,
    didn't I?
T12:   We don't have to talk about him
    specifically. I'm asking about you.
    Whether or not being around that
    relationship brings you any comfort.
    There's nothing wrong with it if it
    does.
C11:   I did everything I could for
    Christopher. Ya' hear me? I got the
    motherfucker that got him. Gave up my
    whole life outta respect for that man,

so don't you sit here tryna guilt trip
    me!
T13:   Okay. You're right. I shouldn't
    have brought it up.
C12:   Nigga, he the one corrupted me!
    Ruined my life over some damn tacos!
    All these gat damn years doin' crime
    and you gon' try to tell me I can't
    pick my own lick?
T13:   Joshua.
C13:   Nigga fuck you! I'm a grown ass
    man! If I wanna cut a nigga's nuts off
    that's my God damn right!
T14:   Joshua, remember who your talking
    to.
C14:   How 'bout that bitch in the house
    on 6th street, huh. You wanted to do
    what you wanted to do, I aint say not
    nare motherfuckin' word! Did I?!
T15:   Joshua, sit down!
C15:   Not nare motherfuckin' word, nigga!
    Don't nobody wanna see that shit!
T16:   If you don't calm down—
C16:   Nigga, how bout I cut yo'
    motherfuckin' nuts off then, huh?!
T17:   Guards!

**Security was able to remand the patient
and secure him via straight jacket. At
this time Dr. Seller was given the option
to conclude the session. He chose to
continue.**

T18:   Alright now, Joshua. Would you like
    to continue?
C17:   Fuck you!
T19:   I can always have you taken back to
    your cell.

No response.

T20:   Joshua?
C18:   I'm fine man. Go 'head ask ya' dumb
    ass questions.
T21:   All of my questions are for your
    benefit, Joshua. You know that.
C19:   Just quit tellin' me what I know,
    aight?
T22:   Well it matters whether or not
    you're going to be cooperative.
C20:   Motherfucker, my arms is buckled to
    a god damn chair, how uncooperative can
    I be?
T23:   (sigh) Alright. The campus church.
    They do bible study on Tuesday's and
    Thursdays and I wonder if you wouldn't
    be interested in joining them sometime?
C21:   You wonder if I wouldn't? The fuck
    kinda question is that?
T24:   Joshua.
C22:   No The fuck I wouldn't be
    interested, aight? I don't believe in
    none of that shit now way.
T25:   I know that's not true.
C23:   So now I'm a liar?
T26:   No. But we've talked before about
    your relationship with God. I know
    there are things you probably need to
    work out.
C24:   That don't mean Im'a be followin'
    some damn institution like a fool.
T27:   It's not an institution. It's just
    a few people looking to strengthen
    their connection with God.
C25:   Is God gonna be there? Nigga fuck a
    connection. You just told me if I

didn't talk you was gonna send me back
to my fuckin' cell. So how 'bout you
work on strengthening your connection
with me while I ignore yo' ass, how's
that sound, huh? Yeah I'll sit here act
like you don't fuckin' exist, and you
can sit here and interpret my fuckin'
farts. Then go sit in a gat damn jerk
circle and tell ya' friends how I work
in mysterious ways.

T28:   Okay. Fair enough. So you want to
talk to God? Directly?

No response.

T29:   What do you think you would say to
him? If you could

No response.

T30:   You could ask anything you want.
Meaning of life. Why certain things
happen.

No response.

T31:   Joshua? It's getting close to the
end of our session. I think this would
be a good thing for you to get out of
your system. Don't you?

No response.

T32:   Joshua?
C26:   I'd ask him...
T33:   Joshua it's time to go.
C27:   I'd ask... what's the point?

END OF TRANSCRIPT